Born in San Francisco, California, on January 12, 1876, Jack London spent his childhood on California ranches and the streets of Oakland, and his youth on the waters of the San Francisco Bay. While still in his teens, he went to sea and became an oyster pirate and a tramp. Odd jobs in a canning factory, a jute mill, a laundry, as well as a thirty-day stretch in a New York county penitentiary for vagrancy, convinced the young wanderer of the value of an education. He attempted to cram high school and college into a few months of study. In 1897, when gold was discovered in the Klondike, twenty-one-year-old London obtained a grubstake, and hiked and sailed six hundred miles from tidewater to gold fields. He spent a freezing, fruitless winter in the Far North and by spring he was ready to give up the adventure and return home to Oakland to write. In 1900, his collection of short stories, *The Son of the Wolf*, was published by Houghton Mifflin. Two more volumes of Yukon short stories, a juvenile, and a Klondike novel followed in rapid succession. Then, in 1903, came his bestselling novel, *The Call of the Wild*, and the beginning of the years which were to bring him wealth and worldwide popularity. In 1904, he went as a war correspondent to Japan, and, in 1914, to Mexico. The eternal traveler, he also cruised the Caribbean and sailed his own ketch to the Solomons before his death in 1916.

Clarice Stasz is a professor of history at Sonoma State University, Californi~~~~ biography of Jack an~~~~

John Barleycorn

Or,
Alcoholic Memoirs

JACK LONDON

Introduction by
Clarice Stasz

A SIGNET CLASSIC

SIGNET CLASSIC
Published by the Penguin Group
Penguin Books USA Inc., 375 Hudson Street,
New York, New York 10014, U.S.A.
Penguin Books Ltd, 27 Wrights Lane, London W8 5TZ, England
Penguin Books Australia Ltd, Ringwood, Victoria, Australia
Penguin Books Canada Ltd, 2801 John Street, Markham,
Ontario, Canada L3R 1B4
Penguin Books (N.Z.) Ltd, 182–190 Wairau Road,
Auckland 10, New Zealand

Penguin Books Ltd, Registered Offices:
Harmondsworth, Middlesex, England

First Signet Classic Printing, May, 1990
10 9 8 7 6 5 4 3 2 1

 REGISTERED TRADEMARK—MARCA REGISTRADA

Library of Congress Catalog Card Number: 89-63818

Printed in the United States of America

Introduction

First-edition collectors need little searching to add *John Barleycorn* to their shelves. It was not only a best-seller in 1913, it was serialized in the *Saturday Evening Post* and made into a movie whose scenes of children in saloons brought out the censors' scissors. This was, after all, the heyday of the Prohibition movement. *John Barleycorn* played a significant role in thrusting that cause toward its goal: an amendment to make alcoholic beverages illegal.

Although London consciously intended the work as propaganda, as in earlier years he had created *The Iron Heel* to warn the public about the dangers of capitalist oligarchy, it survives as much more than a quaint historical document. Indeed, critics known for their disapproval of London in general have described the work as a literary masterpiece. What lifts it to these heights is both its multiplicity of interpretation and its exploration of that most daunting theme, the meaning of life. It is a curious amalgam of confession, sociological commentary, and philosophy. And oddly, though it fails in any one of those categories, its totality is uniquely appealing and satisfying.

What likely most surprises readers familiar with only the mythic Jack London is the very opening page with its discussion of his voting for the suffrage amendment. (Like many Western states, California gave women the vote before the federal government agreed to grant it to their Eastern and Southern sisters.) The mythic Jack London is the archetypal macho sexist alcoholic American writer. Two sources have sketched this caricature. One consists of the many biographers (such as Irving Stone, Richard O'Connor, and Andrew Sinclair) who approached London's life with that prejudice firmly in mind and selected only those facts that seemed to fit it. The other is from most readers' exposure to London being his fiction, notably his Yukon tales or *The Sea Wolf*, stories peopled with tough, aggressive men.

The real Jack London was much more complex. He had a strongly developed "feminine" side, in the Jungian sense of that term. He admired strong, intelligent, talented women and surrounded himself with them. Many of his stories and novels feature women as assertive, vital, and brave as the men, what was known then as New Women. The most significant love of his life, second wife Charmian Kittredge, was a remarkably gutsy and adventurous companion. Though both were outspoken and independent in temperament, they believed such "masculine" virtue must be complemented by nurturance, generosity toward others, and a fostering of the artistic and intuitive. Jack dubbed Charmian his "mate-woman," his partner in life, this when wives and husbands went their separate ways. His friends were much peeved at her interloping!

As one quickly learns in *John Barleycorn*, Jack London became acquainted with liquor and ale in early childhood. His story of carrying a pail of beer to his stepfather, John London, in the field is so poignant that one cannot pass it off easily as invention. We know too from Jack's boyhood friend Frank Atherton that Jack's stepfather took the youngsters to bars, and, while drinking whiskey at home in the evenings, would repeat himself or simply fall asleep mid-sentence. The signs are strong that John London was more than a casual drinker. In his younger days he had been a crafty, capable prairie settler who supported a large family by befriending Indians and borrowing their ways. When his wife died, he took his smallest children and moved to San Francisco, where he married Flora Wellman and welcomed her out-of-wedlock son. His health was not good, and his talents were not fit for city jobs. It is no wonder he went to the saloons and spun stories of past adventures.

Although Jack London more than once wrote inquisitive readers that *John Barleycorn* was not fiction, that it was "bare, bald, absolute fact," its facts are shaped by his strong fictional craft and his sociological bent. His compelling style can lead careless readers to misconstrue the frequency and extent of his drinking. These influences are particularly apparent in his descriptions of adolescent boozing. He ingratiates the reader with his tales of being a kind of Peck's Bad Boy. However, he was fifteen before he tried out the delinquency of oyster pirating. Up to that time he showed himself to be an earnest and obedient student in school, a hard-working youth who sought part-time jobs to help his family out. He was already the budding autodidact and well-known among both librarians and patrons at the Oakland Library.

In chapters nine and ten London astutely analyzes the role of the saloon in shaping male identity. This was a hard period in American culture for men with regard to feeling secure about their roles in life. On the one hand, Teddy Roosevelt and the mass media had fostered the myth of the tough, physically courageous man, while increasingly men were working in offices and organizations. It is not a coincidence that the Boy Scouts and spectator sports took off during this period.

The factory men in Jack London's Oakland faced periods of uncertain employment interspersed with sixteen-hour workdays in dirty, dangerous factories. The saloon provided them rituals surrounding alcohol to win their "manhood's spurs."

As an adolescent striking out for adult status, young Jack complied, all the while despising the routine. Decades later sociologist Howard S. Becker would reveal that, as Jack described, drugs are discomfiting at first try, that the user has to be taught to perceive their effects as pleasurable. Young Jack understood this process. Still, though he saw through the game, he was ashamed of his avoiding it and was unable throughout most of his life to resist the pressures from male peers to down one more.

London was prescient in proposing that two kinds of alcoholism existed, one hereditary, the other acquired. His case was the latter, he argues, for he had "no organic, chemical predispositions" toward the substance. Since Prohibition would remove the social pressures that nurture desire for alcohol in young men, alcoholism can be virtually eliminated, he predicted. It is only in the past decade that research has corroborated London's thesis. Investigators have found differences in the behavior patterns of alcoholics whose family line exhibits the addiction and those from families that don't. Interestingly, London expressed more of the syndrome of the nonfamilial alcoholic, namely a proclivity for depression and drinking under stress.

Of much dispute among London scholars is whether Jack London should even be called an alcoholic. He recounts, for example, long stretches of time without drinking, implying he was always in control, hence could not have been addicted to the stuff. (Besides, he keeps reminding, he never did acquire a taste for it.) He was by no means a day-in and day-out drinker.

On the other hand, Charmian's diaries and his own admissions suggest he was an alcoholic as professionals use the term today. Most notably, when he drank or abstained was easy to predict, as *John Barleycorn* shows. He abstained on long sea voyages, whether on the sealing ship *Sophie Sutherland* or on his trip across the Pacific. On the ranch, he drank only later in the day, once his writing was done. In the city or with certain friends he drank heavily, and sometimes became argumentative, provocative, and downright nasty to those around him. He could be called a situational alcoholic or a binge drinker.

Another characteristic of alcoholism is the development of tolerance, which he documents well in chapter thirty-four. He says his friends never saw him drunk, and many testified to that fact. He learned to order two drinks at once at bars. As this heavy drinking escalated, his old depression was aroused, and he required more liquor to quiet it. "Alcohol tells truth, but its truth is not normal," he warns.

Denial is a psychological trait common to alcoholism. Here London is ambiguous. Chapter thirty concludes, "Oh, I was thoroughly master of myself, and of John Barleycorn." London means this boast ironically, however, for subsequent chapters recount the seductive trickery of drink on the mind. Yet by the end of the book he avers he has beat John Barleycorn, that he was never a drunkard and saw no reason to reform. He admits alcohol has been destructive, but thinks he has won the last round.

Contemporary alcohol experts can point to another feature of his disability, Charmian's attitude toward his behavior. She too denied his alcoholism, both during the time and after his death when she wrote *The Book of Jack London*. She repeatedly claimed he was no dipsomaniac, that charming word for the disease in those days. This refusal to admit the drinking or confront the drinker is now understood to be a common response of family members. This covering-up exists in claims the drinker has a "tiny problem," a "delicate condition," or "can really control himself."

John Barleycorn was written following the worst of London's alcoholic periods. It was a visit to New York that provoked London's apologia. Jack told Charmian he wanted one last fling there before they set off on a trip around the Horn, the last voyage of the noted steel-hulled sailing ship, the *Dirigo*. In New York, he spoke on behalf of woman's suffrage. He also made long disappearances with fellow artists, writers, and editors. Meanwhile, Charmian fumed in their rented rooms or found escape with anarchist Emma Goldman, who comforted her with presents of flowers and diverting trips out of the city. Jack was on the biggest bender of his life. For several days he repented, promised to behave, then went off again for another spree.

When the time came for the *Dirigo* finally to depart, he shaved his head as a form of penance and supplication. That sight only repulsed Charmian and she boarded the ship aggrieved, angry, and close to giving up on the relationship. As he notes in *John Barleycorn*, London did not drink that entire one hundred and forty-eight days. Several weeks into the journey Charmian once again reopened her heart, as she had following his previous, less disruptive stints. The familiar intimacy returned, and she became pregnant with a child she would later miscarry.

At the conclusion of *John Barleycorn*, London proclaims he will not stop drinking. He could not imagine traveling about the world without a glass in hand, as he had in the past. Yet this is not what happened. In fact, he cut back his alcohol consumption considerably, and for a while he lent his name and assistance to a grape juice product being pushed by the prohibitionists.

His abstinence was assisted by failing health. From this time one can trace in Charmian's diaries the clear and steady deterioration of his kidneys. The possible sources of this eventually fatal disease are several and still in dispute: damage from the arsenic- and mercury-based medicines he took for various ailments, the side effect of a tropical disease like malaria, or perhaps even lupus. Whatever, he returned to the ranch a renewed man who tempered his habit, and Charmian no longer penned distressful scenes in her tiny diary.

He had in a way done what Alcoholics Anonymous observes of those who turn to recovery; he had hit bottom. In the three years leading up to this episode, Charmian's only full-term child died following delivery, and she almost died as well; his dream of Wolf House burnt down just as they were ready to move in; and his first wife escalated her manipulations to keep him from his daughters. These tragedies, combined with business losses and problems with publishers, fed his natural pessimism. As he notes in the final, often elegaic chapters, he confronted the Noseless One, the specter of death, with its White Logic that proclaims life to be meaningless. "Our life's a cheat, our death a black abyss."

The White Logic is the final gasp of London's materialism, a philosophy developed during his youthful years of study of philosophy and reinforced by his observations of brutality and oppression toward the working class. It led to the Long Sickness, a period of depression during 1904, which he escaped through commitment to "the PEOPLE," socialism, and Charmian. By 1913, however, he was growing critical of changes in socialism, especially the tendency to have professional leaders make decisions for the workers. He wisely foresaw that this development could as much disempower and abuse the workers as the system the socialists sought to overturn. And though he had not lost his love for Charmian, he had become preoccupied with work and other troubles, that she could not provide the solace from the White Logic she once had given.

Though London's vision of the White Logic is bleak and unrelenting, it did not remain. Hints of change are found near the close of his story, when he suddenly disarms the apparition by proclaiming "hedonism has no meaning." For a moment he sees "that still are mine the possibilities and powers which life and the books had taught me did not exist."

In his final years London was to find a spiritual regeneration and guidepost in modern psychology. Although he read Freud with some interest, it was Carl Jung, whose works were also just being translated, who excited him and gave him a way of answering the Noseless One. In his final short stories, which appeared in *On the Makaloa Mat*, he invoked such symbols as rebirth and the return to the Great Mother. In his copy of Jung he underscored Jesus' words to Nicodemus, "Think not carnally or thou art carnal, but think symbolically and thou art spirit."

Jack London died of uremic poisoning on November 22, 1916, following months of physical suffering and fearless self-exploration. He had traveled enormous distances from the cocky pessimist of John Barleycorn, but this should not be surprising, for after all, the Noseless One is itself an expression of spiritual force, the Knight of Darkness. What he did following completion of this book was allow his worldview to incorporate and eventually make dominant the forces of light. He died in a state of optimism and hope.

His immediate goal for *John Barleycorn* came with the passage of the Eighteenth Amendment in 1919. This experiment brought unhappy consequences both in the growth of organized crime and a massive empowerment of police and intelligence agencies. Historians and sociologists generally interpret Prohibition a failure. Yet it did accomplish its purpose, for alcohol-related diseases fell in incidence, along with the accompanying social problems to family and community, such as domestic violence, desertion, and divorce. Alcohol-related auto accidents dropped by forty percent. Jack London would have believed these reductions in private pain worth the experiment.

—Clarice Stasz

Chapter I

IT ALL came to me one election day. It was on a warm California afternoon, and I had ridden down into the Valley of the Moon from the ranch to the little village to vote yes and no to a host of proposed amendments to the Constitution of the State of California. Because of the warmth of the day I had had several drinks before casting my ballot, and divers drinks after casting it. Then I had ridden up through the vine-clad hills and rolling pastures of the ranch and arrived at the farmhouse in time for another drink and supper.

"How did you vote on the suffrage amendment?" Charmian asked.

"I voted for it."

She uttered an exclamation of surprise. For be it known, in my younger days, despite my ardent democracy, I had been opposed to woman suffrage. In my later and more tolerant years I had been unenthusiastic in my acceptance of it as an inevitable social phenomenon.

"Now just why did you vote for it?" Charmian asked.

I answered. I answered at length. I answered indignantly. The more I answered, the more indignant I became. (No; I was not drunk. The horse I had ridden was well-named "The Outlaw." I'd like to see any drunken man ride her.)

And yet—how shall I say?—I was lighted up, I was feeling "good," I was pleasantly jingled.

14

"When the women get the ballot, they will vote for prohibition," I said. "It is the wives, and sisters, and mothers, and they only, who will drive the nails into the coffin of John Barleycorn—"

"But I thought you were a friend to John Barleycorn," Charmian interpolated.

"I am. I was. I am not. I never am. I am never less his friend than when he is with me and when I seem most his friend. He is the king of liars. He is the frankest truth-sayer. He is the august companion with whom one walks with the gods. He is also in league with the Noseless One. His way leads to truth naked, and to death. He gives clear vision, and muddy dreams. He is the enemy of life, and the teacher of wisdom beyond life's vision. He is a red-handed killer, and he slays youth."

And Charmian looked at me, and I knew she wondered where I had got it.

I continued to talk. As I say, I was lighted up. In my brain every thought was at home. Every thought, in its little cell, crouched ready-dressed at the door, like prisoners at midnight waiting a jail-break. And every thought was a vision, bright-imaged, sharp-cut, unmistakable. My brain was illuminated by the clear, white light of alcohol. John Barleycorn was on a truth-telling rampage, giving away the choicest secrets on himself. And I was his spokesman. There moved the multitudes of memories of my past life, all orderly arranged like soldiers in some vast review. It was mine to pick and choose. I was a lord of thought, the master of my vocabulary and of the totality of my experience, unerringly capable of selecting my data and building my exposition. For so John Barleycorn tricks and lures, setting the maggots of intelligence gnawing, whispering his fatal intuitions of truth, flinging purple passages into the monotony of one's days.

I outlined my life to Charmian, and expounded

the make-up of my constitution. I was no hereditary alcoholic. I had been born with no organic,
chemical predisposition toward alcohol. In this
matter I was normal in my generation. Alcohol
was an acquired taste. It had been painfully acquired. Alcohol had been a dreadfully repugnant
thing—more nauseous than any physic. Even now
I did not like the taste of it. I drank it only for its
"kick." And from the age of five to that of twenty-
five, I had not learned to care for its kick. Twenty
years of unwilling apprenticeship had been required to make my system rebelliously tolerant of
alcohol, to make me, in the heart and the deeps of
me, desirous of alcohol.

I sketched my first contacts with alcohol, told of
my first intoxications and revulsions, and pointed
out always the one thing that in the end had won
me over—namely, the accessibility of alcohol. Not
only had it always been accessible, but every interest of my developing life had drawn me to it. A
newsboy on the streets, a sailor, a miner, a wanderer in far lands, always where men came together to exchange ideas, to laugh and boast and
dare, to relax, to forget the dull toil of tiresome
nights and days, always they came together over
alcohol. The saloon was the place of congregation.
Men gathered to it as primitive men gathered
about the fire of the squatting-place or the fire at
the mouth of the cave.

I reminded Charmian of the canoe-houses from
which she had been barred in the South Pacific,
where the kinky-haired cannibals escaped from
their womenkind and feasted and drank by themselves, the sacred precincts taboo to women under pain of death. As a youth, by way of the
saloon I had escaped from the narrowness of wom-
en's influence into the wide free world of men.
All ways led to the saloon. The thousand roads of

romance and adventure drew together in the saloon, and thence led out and on over the world.

"The point is," I concluded my sermon, "that it is the accessibility of alcohol that has given me my taste for alcohol. I did not care for it. I used to laugh at it. Yet here I am, at the last, possessed with the drinker's desire. It took twenty years to implant that desire; and for ten years more that desire has grown. And the effect of satisfying that desire is anything but good. Temperamentally I am wholesome-hearted and merry. Yet when I walk with John Barleycorn I suffer all the damnation of intellectual pessimism.

"—But," I hastened to add (I always hasten to add), "—John Barleycorn must have his due. He does tell the truth. That is the curse of it. The so-called truths of life are not true. They are the vital lies by which life lives, and John Barleycorn gives them the lie."

"Which does not make toward life," Charmian said.

"Very true," I answered. "And that is the perfectest hell of it. John Barleycorn makes toward death. That is why I voted for the amendment to-day. I read back in my life and saw how the accessibility of alcohol had given me the taste for it. You see, comparatively few alcoholics are born in a generation. And by alcoholic I mean a man whose chemistry craves alcohol and drives him resistlessly to it. The great majority of habitual drinkers are born not only without desire for alcohol but with actual repugnance toward it. Not the first, nor the twentieth, nor the hundredth drink, succeeded in giving them the liking. But they learned, just as men learn to smoke; though it is far easier to learn to smoke than to learn to drink. They learned because alcohol was so accessible. The women know the game. They pay for it—the wives and sisters and mothers. And when they

come to vote they will vote for prohibition. And
the best of it is that there will be no hardship
worked on the coming generation. Not having
access to alcohol, not being predisposed toward
alcohol, it will never miss alcohol. It will mean life
more abundant for the manhood of the young
boys born and growing up—ay, and life more
abundant for the young girls born and growing
up to share the lives of the young men."

"Why not write all this up for the sake of the
young men and women coming?" Charmian asked.
"Why not write it so as to help the wives and
sisters and mothers to the way they should vote?"

"The 'Memoirs of an Alcoholic,' " I sneered—or,
rather John Barleycorn sneered; for he sat with me
there at table in my pleasant, philanthropic jingle,
and it is a trick of John Barleycorn to turn the
smile to a sneer without an instant's warning.

"No," said Charmian, ignoring John Barleycorn's
roughness as so many women have learned to do.
"You have shown yourself no alcoholic, no dipsomaniac, but merely an habitual drinker, one who
has made John Barleycorn's acquaintance through
long years of rubbing shoulders with him. Write it
up and call it 'Alcoholic Memoirs.' "

Chapter II

AND, ere I begin, I must ask the reader to walk with me in all sympathy; and, since sympathy is merely understanding, begin by understanding me and whom and what I write about. In the first place, I am a seasoned drinker. I have no constitutional predisposition for alcohol. I am not stupid. I am not a swine. I know the drinking game from A to Zed, and I have used my judgment in drinking. I never have to be put to bed. Nor do I stagger. In short, I am a normal, average man; and I drink in the normal, average way, as drinking goes. And this is the very point: I am writing of the effects of alcohol on the normal, average man. I have no word to say for or about the microscopically unimportant excessivist, the dipsomaniac.

There are, broadly speaking, two types of drinkers. There is the man whom we all know, stupid, unimaginative, whose brain is bitten numbly by numb maggots; who walks generously with widespread, tentative legs, falls frequently in the gutter, and who sees, in the extremity of his ecstasy, blue mice and pink elephants. He is the type that gives rise to the jokes in the funny papers.

The other type of drinker has imagination, vision. Even when most pleasantly jingled he walks straight and naturally, never staggers nor falls, and knows just where he is and what he is doing. It is not his body but his brain that is drunken. He may bubble with wit, or expand with good fellowship. Or he may see intellectual specters and phantoms that are cosmic and logical and that take the forms of syllogisms. It is when in this condition that he strips away the husks of life's healthiest illusions and gravely considers the iron collar of necessity welded about the neck of his soul. This is the hour of John Barleycorn's subtlest power. It is easy for any man to roll in the gutter. But it is a terrible ordeal for a man to stand upright on his two legs unswaying, and decide that in all the universe he finds for himself but one freedom, namely, the anticipating of the day of his death. With this man this is the hour of the white logic (of which more anon), when he knows that he may know only the laws of things—the meaning of things never. This is his danger hour. His feet are taking hold of the path that leads down into the grave.

All is clear to him. All these baffling head-reaches after immortality are but the panics of souls frightened by the fear of death, and cursed with the thrice-cursed gift of imagination. They have not the instinct of death; they lack the will to die when the time to die is at hand. They trick themselves into believing they will outwit the game and win to a future, leaving the other animals to the darkness of the grave or the annihilating heats of the crematory. But he, this man in the hour of his white logic, knows that they trick and outwit themselves. The one event happeneth to all alike. There is no new thing under the sun, not even that yearned-for bauble of feeble souls—immortality. But he knows, *he* knows, standing upright on his two legs unswaying. He is compounded of meat and wine and sparkle, of sun-mote and world-dust, a frail mechanism made to run for a span, to be tinkered at by doctors of divinity and doctors of physic, and to be flung into the scrap-heap at the end.

Of course, all this is soul-sickness, life-sickness. It is the penalty the imaginative man must pay for his friendship with John Barleycorn. The penalty paid by the stupid man is simpler, easier. He drinks himself into sottish unconsciousness. He sleeps a drugged sleep, and, if he dream, his dreams are dim and inarticulate. But to the imaginative man, John Barleycorn sends the pitiless, spectral syllogisms of the white logic. He looks upon life and all its affairs with the jaundiced eye of a pessimistic German philosopher. He sees through all illusions. He trans-values all values. God is bad, truth is a cheat, and life is a joke. From his calm-mad heights, with the certitude of a god, he beholds all life as evil. Wife, children, friends—in the clear, white light of his logic they are exposed as frauds and shams. He sees through them, and all that he sees is their frailty, their meagerness, their sordidness, their pitifulness. No longer do they fool him. They are miserable little egotisms, like all the other little humans, fluttering their May-fly life-dance of an hour. They are without freedom. They are puppets of chance. So is he. He realizes that. But there is one difference. He sees; he knows. And he knows his one freedom: he may anticipate the day of his death. All of which is not good for a man who is made to live and love and be loved. Yet suicide, quick or slow, a sudden spill or a gradual oozing away through the years, is the price John Barleycorn exacts. No friend of his ever escapes making the just, due payment.

Chapter III

I WAS five years old the first time I got drunk. It was on a hot day, and my father was plowing in the field. I was sent from the house, half a mile away, to carry to him a pail of beer. "And be sure you don't spill it," was the parting injunction.

It was, as I remember it, a lard pail, very wide across the top, and without a cover. As I toddled along, the beer slopped over the rim upon my legs. And as I toddled, I pondered. Beer was a very precious thing. Come to think of it, it must be wonderfully good. Else why was I never permitted to drink of it in the house? Other things kept from me by the grown-ups I had found good. Then this, too, was good. Trust the grown-ups. They knew. And anyway, the pail was too full. I was slopping it against my legs and spilling it on the ground. Why waste it? And no one would know whether I had drunk or spilled it.

I was so small that in order to negotiate the pail, I sat down and gathered it into my lap. First I sipped the foam. I was disappointed. The preciousness evaded me. Evidently it did not reside in the foam. Besides, the taste was not good. Then I remembered seeing the grown-ups blow the foam away before they drank. I buried my face in the foam and lapped the solid liquid beneath. It was n't good at all. But still I drank. The grown-ups knew what they were about. Considering my diminutiveness, the size of the pail in my lap, and my drinking out of it with my breath held and my face buried to the ears in foam, it was rather difficult to estimate how much I drank. Also, I was gulping it down like medicine, in nauseous haste to get the ordeal over.

I shuddered when I started on, and decided that the good taste would come afterward. I tried several times more in the course of that long half-mile. Then, astounded by the quantity of beer that was lacking, and remembering having seen stale beer made to foam afresh, I took a stick and stirred what was left till it foamed to the brim.

And my father never noticed. He emptied the pail with the wide thirst of the sweating plow-man, returned it to me, and started up the plow. I endeavored to walk beside the horses. I remember tottering and falling against their heels in front of the shining share, and that my father hauled back on the lines so violently that the horses nearly sat down on me. He told me afterward that it was by only a matter of inches that I escaped disembowelling. Vaguely, too, I remember, my father carried me in his arms to the trees on the edge of the field, while all the world reeled and swung about me and I was aware of deadly nausea mingled with an appalling conviction of sin.

I slept the afternoon away under the trees, and when my father roused me at sundown it was a very sick little boy that got up and dragged wearily homeward. I was exhausted, oppressed by the weight of my limbs, and in my stomach was a harp-like vibration that extended to my throat and brain. My condition was like that of one who had gone through a battle with poison. In truth, I had been poisoned.

In the weeks and months that followed I had no more interest in beer than in the kitchen stove after it had burned me. The grown-ups were right. Beer was not for children. The grown-ups did n't mind it; but neither did they mind taking pills and castor oil. As for me, I could manage to get along quite well without beer. Yes, and to the day of my death I could have managed to get along quite well without it. But circumstance decreed otherwise. At every turn in the world in which I lived, John Barleycorn beckoned. There was no escaping him. All paths led to him. And it took twenty years of contact, of exchanging greetings and passing on with my tongue in my cheek, to develop in me a sneaking liking for the rascal.

Chapter IV

MY NEXT BOUT with John Barleycorn occurred when I was seven. This time my imagination was at fault, and I was frightened into the encounter. Still farming, my family had moved to a ranch on the bleak sad coast of San Mateo County south of San Francisco. It was a wild, primitive countryside in those days; and often I heard my mother pride herself that we were old American stock and not immigrant Irish and Italians like our neighbors. In all our section there was only one other old American family.

One Sunday morning found me, how or why I cannot now remember, at the Morrisey ranch. A number of young people had gathered there from the nearer ranches. Besides, the oldsters had been there, drinking since early dawn, and, some of them, since the night before. The Morriseys were a huge breed, and there were many strapping great sons and uncles, heavy-booted, big-fisted, rough-voiced.

Suddenly there were screams from the girls and cries of "Fight!" There was a rush. Men hurled themselves out of the kitchen. Two giants, flush-faced, with graying hair, were locked in each other's arms. One was Black Matt, who, everybody said, had killed two men in his time. The women screamed softly, crossed themselves, or prayed brokenly, hiding their eyes and peeping through their fingers. But not I. It is a fair presumption that I was the most interested spectator. Maybe I would see that wonderful thing, a man killed. Anyway, I would see a man-fight. Great was my disappointment. Black Matt and Tom Morrisey merely held on to each other and lifted their clumsy-booted feet in what seemed a grotesque, elephantine dance. They were too drunk to fight. Then the peacemakers got hold of them and led them back to cement the new friendship in the kitchen.

Soon they were all talking at once, rumbling and roaring as big-chested open-air men will when whisky has whipped their taciturnity. And I, a little shaver of seven, my heart in my mouth, my trembling body strung tense as a deer's on the verge of flight, peered wonderingly in at the open door and learned more of the strangeness of men. And I marveled at Black Matt and Tom Morrisey, sprawled over the table, arms about each other's necks, weeping lovingly.

The kitchen-drinking continued, and the girls outside grew timorous. They knew the drink game, and all were certain that something terrible was going to happen. They protested that they did not wish to be there when it happened, and some one suggested going to a big Italian rancho four miles away, where they could get up a dance. Immediately they paired off, lad and lassie, and started down the sandy road. And each lad walked with his sweetheart—trust a child of seven to listen and to know the love affairs of his countryside. And behold, I, too, was a lad with a lassie. A little Irish girl of my own age had been paired off with me. We were the only children in this spontaneous affair. Perhaps the oldest couple might have been twenty. There were chits of girls, quite grown up, of fourteen and sixteen, walking with their fellows. But we were uniquely young, this little Irish girl and I, and we walked hand in hand,

and, sometimes, under the tutelage of our elders, with my arm around her waist. Only that was n't comfortable. And I was very proud, on that bright Sunday morning, going down the long bleak road among the sandhills. I, too, had my girl, and was a little man.

The Italian rancho was a bachelor establishment. Our visit was hailed with delight. The red wine was poured in tumblers for all, and the long dining-room was partly cleared for dancing. And the young fellows drank and danced with the girls to the strains of an accordeon. To me that music was divine. I had never heard anything so glorious. The young Italian who furnished it would even get up and dance, his arms around his girl, playing the accordeon behind her back. All of which was very wonderful for me, who did not dance, but who sat at a table and gazed wide-eyed at the amazingness of life. I was only a little lad, and there was so much of life for me to learn. As the time passed, the Irish lads began helping them-selves to the wine, and jollity and high spirits reigned. I noted that some of them staggered and fell down in the dances, and that one had gone to sleep in a corner. Also, some of the girls were complaining and wanting to leave, and others of the girls were titteringly complacent, willing for anything to happen.

When our Italian hosts had offered me wine in a general sort of way, I had declined. My beer experience had been enough for me, and I had no inclination to traffic further in the stuff nor in anything related to it. Unfortunately, one young Italian, Peter, an impish soul, seeing me sitting solitary, stirred by a whim of the moment, half-filled a tumbler with wine and passed it to me. He was sitting across the table from me. I declined. His face grew stern, and he insistently proffered the wine. And then terror descended upon me—a terror which I must explain.

My mother had theories. First, she steadfastly maintained that brunettes and all the tribe of dark-eyed humans were deceitful. Needless to say, my mother was a blond. Next, she was convinced that the dark-eyed Latin races were profoundly sensitive, profoundly treacherous, and profoundly murderous. Again and again, drinking in the strangeness and the fearsomeness of the world from her lips, I had heard her state that if one offended an Italian, no matter how slightly and unintentionally, he was certain to retaliate by stabbing one in the back. That was her particular phrase—"stab you in the back."

Now, although I had been eager to see Black Matt kill Tom Morrisey that morning, I did not care to furnish to the dancers the spectacle of a knife sticking in *my* back. I had not yet learned to distinguish between facts and theories. My faith was implicit in my mother's exposition of the Italian character. Besides, I had some glimmering inkling of the sacredness of hospitality. Here was a treacherous, sensitive, murderous Italian, offering me hospitality. I had been taught to believe that if I offended him he would strike at me with a knife precisely as a horse kicked out when one got too close to its heels and worried it. Then, too, this Italian, Peter, had those terrible black eyes I had heard my mother talk about. They were eyes different from the eyes I knew, from the blues and grays and hazels of my own family, from the pale and genial blues of the Irish. Perhaps Peter had had a few drinks. At any rate his eyes were brilliantly black and sparkling with deviltry. They were the mysterious, the unknown, and who was I, a seven-year-old, to analyze them and know their prankishness? In them I visioned sudden death, and I declined the wine half-heartedly. The expression in his eyes changed. They grew stern and imperious as he shoved the tumbler of wine closer.

What could I do? I have faced real death since in my life, but never have I known the fear of death as I knew it then. I put the glass to my lips, and Peter's eyes relented. I knew he would not kill me just then. That was a relief. But the wine was not. It was cheap, new wine, bitter and sour, made of the leavings and scrapings of the vineyards and the vats, and it tasted far worse than beer. There is only one way to take medicine, and that is to take it. And that is the way I took that wine. I threw my head back and gulped it down. I had to gulp again and hold the poison down, for poison it was to my child's tissues and membranes.

Looking back now, I can realize that Peter was astounded. He half-filled a second tumbler and shoved it across the table. Frozen with fear, in despair at the fate which had befallen me, I gulped the second glass down like the first. This was too much for Peter. He must share the infant prodigy he had discovered. He called Dominick, a young mustached Italian, to see the sight. This time it was a full tumbler that was given to me. One will do anything to live. I gripped myself, mastered the qualms that rose in my throat, and downed the stuff.

Dominick had never seen an infant of such heroic caliber. Twice again he refilled the tumbler, each time to the brim, and watched it disappear down my throat. By this time my exploits were attracting attention. Middle-aged Italian laborers, old-country peasants who did not talk English and who could not dance with the Irish girls, surrounded me. They were swarthy and wild-looking; they wore belts and red shirts; and I knew they carried knives; and they ringed me around like a pirate chorus. And Peter and Dominick made me show off for them.

Had I lacked imagination, had I been stupid, had I been stubbornly mulish in having my own way, I should never have got in this pickle. And the lads and lassies were dancing, and there was no one to save me from my fate. How much I drank I do not know. My memory of it is of an age-long suffering of fear in the midst of a murderous crew, and of an infinite number of glasses of red wine passing across the bare boards of a wine-drenched table and going down my burning throat. Bad as the wine was, a knife in the back was worse, and I must survive at any cost.

Looking back with the drinker's knowledge, I know now why I did not collapse stupefied upon the table. As I have said, I was frozen, I was paralyzed, with fear. The only movement I made was to convey that never-ending procession of glasses to my lips. I was a poised and motionless receptacle for all that quantity of wine. It lay inert in my fear-inert stomach. I was too frightened, even, for my stomach to turn. So all that Italian crew looked on and marveled at the infant phenomenon that downed wine with the *sang-froid* of an automaton. It is not in the spirit of braggadocio that I dare to assert they had never seen anything like it.

The time came to go. The tipsy antics of the lads had led a majority of the soberer-minded lassies to compel a departure. I found myself at the door, beside my little maiden. She had not had my experience, so she was sober. She was fascinated by the titubations of the lads who strove to walk beside their girls, and began to mimic them. I thought this a great game, and I, too, began to stagger tipsily. But she had no wine to stir up, while my movements quickly set the fumes rising to my head. Even at the start, I was more

realistic than she. In several minutes I was astonishing myself. I saw one lad, after reeling half a
dozen steps, pause at the side of the road, gravely
peer into the ditch, and gravely, and after apparent deep thought, fall into it. To me this was
excruciatingly funny. I staggered to the edge of
the ditch, fully intending to stop on the edge. I
came to myself, in the ditch, in process of being
hauled out by several anxious-faced girls.

I did n't care to play at being drunk any more.
There was no more fun in me. My eyes were
beginning to swim, and with wide-open mouth I
panted for air. A girl led me by the hand on either
side, but my legs were leaden. The alcohol I had
drunk was striking my heart and brain like a club.
Had I been a weakling of a child, I am confident
that it would have killed me. As it was, I know I
was nearer death than any of the scared girls
dreamed. I could hear them bickering among themselves as to whose fault it was; some were weeping
—for themselves, for me, and for the disgraceful
way their lads had behaved. But I was not interested. I was suffocating, and I wanted air. To
move was agony. It made me pant harder. Yet
those girls persisted in making me walk, and it
was four miles home. Four miles! I remember my
swimming eyes saw a small bridge across the road
an infinite distance away. In fact, it was not a
hundred feet distant. When I reached it, I sank
down and lay on my back panting. The girls tried
to lift me, but I was helpless and suffocating.
Their cries of alarm brought Larry, a drunken
youth of seventeen, who proceeded to resuscitate
me by jumping on my chest. Dimly I remember
this, and the squalling of the girls as they struggled with him and dragged him away. And then
I knew nothing, though I learned afterward that
Larry wound up under the bridge and spent the
night there.

When I came to, it was dark. I had been carried unconscious for four miles and been put to bed. I was a sick child, and, despite the terrible strain on my heart and tissues, I continually relapsed into the madness of delirium. All the content of the terrible and horrible in my child's mind spilled out. The most frightful visions were realities to me. I saw murders committed, and I was pursued by murderers. I screamed and raved and fought. My sufferings were prodigious. Emerging from such delirium, I would hear my mother's voice: "But the child's brain. He will lose his reason." And sinking back into delirium, I would take the idea with me and be immured in madhouses, and be beaten by keepers, and surrounded by screeching lunatics.

One thing that had strongly impressed my young mind was the talk of my elders about the dens of iniquity in San Francisco's Chinatown. In my delirium I wandered deep beneath the ground through a thousand of these dens, and behind locked doors of iron I suffered and died a thousand deaths. And when I would come upon my father, seated at table in these subterranean crypts, gambling with Chinese for great stakes of gold, all my outrage gave vent in the vilest cursing. I would rise in bed, struggling against the detaining hands, and curse my father till the rafters rang. All the inconceivable filth a child running at large in a primitive countryside may hear men utter, was mine; and though I had never dared utter such oaths, they now poured from me, at the top of my lungs, as I cursed my father sitting there underground and gambling with long-haired, long-nailed Chinamen.

It is a wonder that I did not burst my heart or brain that night. A seven-year-old child's arteries and nerve-centers are scarcely fitted to endure the terrific paroxysms that convulsed me. No one slept in the thin, frame farmhouse that night when John Barleycorn had his will of me. And Larry, under the bridge, had no delirium like mine. I am confident that his sleep was stupefied and dreamless, and that he awoke next day merely to heaviness and moroseness, and that if he lives to-day he does not remember that night, so passing was it as an incident. But my brain was seared forever by that experience. Writing now, thirty years afterward, every vision is as distinct, as sharp-cut, every pain as vital and terrible, as on that night.

I was sick for days afterward, and I needed none of my mother's injunctions to avoid John Barleycorn in the future. My mother had been dreadfully shocked. She held that I had done wrong, very wrong, and that I had gone contrary to all her teaching. And how was I, who was never allowed to talk back, who lacked the very words with which to express my psychology—how was I to tell my mother that it was her teaching that was directly responsible for my drunkenness? Had it not been for her theories about dark eyes and Italian character, I should never have wet my lips with the sour, bitter wine. And not until man-grown did I tell her the true inwardness of that disgraceful affair.

In those after-days of sickness, I was confused on some points, and very clear on others. I felt guilty of sin, yet smarted with a sense of injustice. It had not been my fault; yet I had done wrong. But very clear was my resolution never to touch liquor again. No mad dog was ever more afraid of water than was I of alcohol.

Yet the point I am making is that this experience, terrible as it was, could not in the end deter me from forming John Barleycorn's cheek-by-jowl acquaintance. All about me, even then, were the forces moving me toward him. In the first place, barring my mother, ever extreme in her views, it seemed to me all the grown-ups looked upon the affair with tolerant eyes. It was a joke, something funny that had happened. There was no shame attached. Even the lads and lassies giggled and snickered over their part in the affair, narrating with gusto how Larry had jumped on my chest and slept under the bridge, how So-and-So had slept out in the sandhills that night, and what had happened to the other lad who fell in the ditch. As I say, so far as I could see, there was no shame anywhere. It had been something ticklishly, devilishly fine—a bright and gorgeous episode in the monotony of life and labor on that bleak, fog-girt coast.

The Irish ranchers twitted me good-naturedly on my exploit, and patted me on the back until I felt that I had done something heroic. Peter and Dominick and the other Italians were proud of my drinking prowess. The face of morality was not set against drinking. Besides, everybody drank. There was not a teetotaler in the community. Even the teacher of our little country school, a graying man of fifty, gave us vacations on the occasions when he wrestled with John Barleycorn and was thrown. Thus there was no spiritual deterrence. My loathing for alcohol was purely physiological. I did n't like the damned stuff.

Chapter V

THIS PHYSICAL LOATHING for alcohol I have never got over. But I have conquered it. To this day I re-conquer it every time I take a drink. The palate never ceases to rebel, and the palate can be trusted to know what is good for the body. But men do not knowingly drink for the effect alcohol produces on the body. What they drink for is the brain-effect; and if it must come through the body, so much the worse for the body.

And yes, despite my physical loathing for alcohol, the brightest spots in my child life were the saloons. Sitting on the heavy potato wagons, wrapped in fog, feet stinging from inactivity, the horses plodding slowly along the deep road through the sandhills, one bright vision made the way never too long. The bright vision was the saloon at Colma, where my father, or whoever drove, always got out to get a drink. And I got out to warm by the great stove and get a soda cracker. Just one soda cracker, but a fabulous luxury. Saloons were good for something. Back behind the plodding horses, I would take an hour in consuming that one cracker. I took the smallest of nibbles, never losing a crumb, and chewed the nibble till it became the thinnest and most delectable of pastes. I never voluntarily swallowed this paste. I just tasted it, and went on tasting it, turning it over with my tongue, spreading it on the inside of one cheek, then on the inside of the other cheek, until, at the end, it eluded me and in tiny drops and oozelets slipped and dribbled down my throat. Horace Fletcher had nothing on me when it came to soda crackers.

I liked saloons. Especially I liked the San Francisco saloons. They had the most delicious dainties for the taking—strange breads and crackers, cheeses, sausages, sardines—wonderful foods that I never saw on our meager home-table. And once, I remember, a barkeeper mixed me a sweet temperance drink of syrup and soda water. My father did not pay for it. It was the barkeeper's treat, and he became my ideal of a good, kind man. I dreamed day dreams of him for years. Although I was seven years old at the time, I can see him now with undiminished clearness, though I never laid eyes on him but that one time. The saloon was south of Market Street in San Francisco. It stood on the west side of the street. As you entered, the bar was on the left. On the right, against the wall, was the free-lunch counter. It was a long, narrow room, and at the rear, beyond the beer kegs on tap, were small round tables and chairs. The barkeeper was blue-eyed, and had fair, silky hair peeping out from under a black silk skull-cap. I remember he wore a brown Cardigan jacket, and I know precisely the spot, in the midst of the array of bottles, from which he took the bottle of red-colored syrup. He and my father talked long, and I sipped my sweet drink and worshiped him. And for years afterward I worshiped the memory of him.

Despite my two disastrous experiences, here was John Barleycorn, prevalent and accessible everywhere in the community, luring and drawing me. Here were connotations of the saloon making deep indentations in a child's mind. Here was a child, forming its first judgments of the world, finding the saloon a delightful and desirable place.

Stores, nor public buildings, nor all the dwellings of men ever opened their doors to me and let me warm by their fires or permitted me to eat the food of the gods from narrow shelves against the wall. Their doors were ever closed to me; the saloon's doors were ever open. And always and everywhere I found saloons, on highway and byway, up narrow alleys and on busy thoroughfares, bright-lighted and cheerful, warm in winter and in summer dark and cool. Yes, the saloon was a mighty fine place, and it was more than that.

By the time I was ten years old, my family had abandoned ranching and gone to live in the city. And here, at ten, I began on the streets as a newsboy. One of the reasons for this was that we needed the money. Another reason was that I needed the exercise. I had found my way to the free public library, and was reading myself into nervous prostration. On the poor-ranches on which I had lived there had been no books. In ways truly miraculous, I had been lent four books, marvelous books, and them I had devoured. One was the life of Garfield; the second, Paul du Chaillu's African travels; the third, a novel by Ouida with the last forty pages missing; and the fourth, Irving's "Alhambra." This last had been lent me by a school-teacher. I was not a forward child. Unlike Oliver Twist, I was incapable of asking for more. When I returned the "Alhambra" to the teacher I hoped she would lend me another book. And because she did not—most likely she deemed me unappreciative—I cried all the way home on the three-mile tramp from the school to the ranch. I waited and yearned for her to lend me another book. Scores of times I nerved myself almost to the point of asking her, but never quite reached the necessary pitch of effrontery.

And then came the city of Oakland, and on the shelves of that free-library I discovered all the great world beyond the skyline. Here were thousands of books as good as my four wonder-books, and some were even better. Libraries were not concerned with children in those days, and I had strange adventures. I remember, in the catalogue, being impressed by the title, "The Adventures of Peregrine Pickle." I filled an application blank and the librarian handed me the collected and entirely unexpurgated works of Smollett in one huge volume. I read everything, but principally history and adventure, and all the old travels and voyages. I read mornings, afternoons, and nights. I read in bed, I read at table, I read as I walked to and from school, and I read at recess while the other boys were playing. I began to get the "jerks." To everybody I replied: "Go away. You make me nervous."

And so, at ten, I was out on the streets, a newsboy. I had no time to read. I was busy getting exercise and learning how to fight, busy learning forwardness, and brass and bluff. I had an imagination and a curiosity about all things that made me plastic. Not least among the things I was curious about was the saloon. And I was in and out of many a one. I remember, in those days, on the east side of Broadway between Sixth and Seventh, from corner to corner, there was a solid block of saloons.

In the saloons life was different. Men talked with great voices, laughed great laughs, and there was an atmosphere of greatness. Here was something more than common every-day where nothing happened. Here life was always very live, and sometimes, even lurid, when blows were struck, and blood was shed, and big policemen came shouldering in. Great moments, these, for me, my head filled with all the wild and valiant fighting of the gallant adventures on sea and land. There were no big moments when I trudged along the street throwing my papers in at doors. But in the saloons, even the sots, stupefied, sprawling across the tables or in the sawdust, were objects of mystery and wonder.

And more, the saloons were right. The city fathers sanctioned them and licensed them. They were not the terrible places I heard boys deem them who lacked my opportunities to know. Terrible they might be, but then that only meant they were terribly wonderful, and it is the terribly wonderful that a boy desires to know. In the same way pirates, and shipwrecks, and battles were terrible; and what healthy boy would n't give his immortal soul to participate in such affairs?

Besides, in saloons I saw reporters, editors, lawyers, judges, whose names and faces I knew. They put the seal of social approval on the saloon. They verified my own feeling of fascination in the saloon. They, too, must have found there that something different, that something beyond, which I sensed and groped after. What it was, I did not know; yet there it must be, for there men focused like buzzing flies about a honey pot. I had no sorrows, and the world was very bright, so I could not guess that what these men sought was forgetfulness of jaded toil and stale grief.

Not that I drank at that time. From ten to fifteen I rarely tasted liquor, but I was intimately in contact with drinkers and drinking places. The only reason I did not drink was because I did n't like the stuff. As the time passed, I worked as boy-helper on an ice-wagon, set up pins in a bowling-alley with a saloon attached, and swept out saloons at Sunday picnic grounds.

Big jovial Josie Harper ran a road-house at Telegraph Avenue and Thirty-ninth Street. Here for a year I delivered an evening paper, until my route was changed to the water-front and tenderloin of Oakland. The first month, when I collected Josie

Harper's bill, she poured me a glass of wine. I
was ashamed to refuse, so I drank it. But after
that I watched the chance when she was n't around
so as to collect from her barkeeper.

The first day I worked in the bowling-alley, the
barkeeper, according to custom, called us boys up
to have a drink after we had been setting up pins
for several hours. The others asked for beer. I said
I 'd take ginger ale. The boys snickered, and I
noticed the barkeeper favored me with a strange,
searching scrutiny. Nevertheless he opened a bottle of ginger ale. Afterward, back in the alleys, in
the pauses between games, the boys enlightened
me. I had offended the barkeeper. A bottle of
ginger ale cost the saloon ever so much more than
a glass of steam beer; and it was up to me, if I
wanted to hold my job, to drink beer. Besides,
beer was food. I could work better on it. There
was no food in ginger ale. After that, when I
could n't sneak out of it, I drank beer and wondered what men found in it that was so good. I
was always aware that I was missing something.

What I really liked in those days was candy. For
five cents I could buy five "cannon-balls"—big
lumps of the most delicious lastingness. I could
chew and worry a single one for an hour. Then
there was a Mexican who sold big slabs of brown
chewing-taffy for five cents each. It required a
quarter of a day properly to absorb one of them.
And many a day I made my entire lunch off of
one of those slabs. In truth, I found food there,
but not in beer.

Chapter VI

BUT THE TIME was rapidly drawing near when I was to begin my second series of bouts with John Barleycorn. When I was fourteen, my head filled with the tales of the old voyagers, my vision with tropic isles and far sea-rims, I was sailing a small centerboard skiff around San Francisco Bay and on the Oakland Estuary. I wanted to go to sea. I wanted to get away from monotony and the commonplace. I was in the flower of my adolescence, a-thrill with romance and adventure, dreaming of wild life in the wild man-world. Little I guessed how all the warp and woof of that man-world was entangled with alcohol.

So, one day, as I hoisted sail on my skiff, I met Scotty. He was a husky youngster of seventeen, a runaway apprentice, he told me, from an English ship in Australia. He had just worked his way on another ship to San Francisco; and now he wanted to see about getting a berth on a whaler. Across the estuary, near where the whalers lay, was lying the sloop-yacht *Idler*. The caretaker was a harpooner who intended sailing next voyage on the whale ship *Bonanza*. Would I take him, Scotty, over in my skiff to call upon the harpooner?

Would I? Had n't I heard the stories and rumors about the *Idler*?—the big sloop that had come up from the Sandwich Islands where it had been engaged in smuggling opium. And the harpooner who was caretaker! How often had I seen him and envied him his freedom. He never had to leave the water. He slept aboard the *Idler* each night, while I had to go home upon the land to go to bed. The harpooner was only nineteen years old (and I have never had anything but his own word that he was a harpooner); but he had been too shining and glorious a personality for me ever to address as I paddled around the yacht at a wistful distance. Would I take Scotty, the runaway sailor, to visit the harpooner, on the opium-smuggler *Idler*? Would I!

The harpooner came on deck to answer our hail, and invited us aboard. I played the sailor and the man, fending off the skiff so that it would not mar the yatch's white paint, dropping the skiff astern on a long painter, and making the painter fast with two nonchalant half-hitches. We went below. It was the first sea-interior I had ever seen. The clothing on the wall smelled musty. But what of that? Was it not the sea-gear of men? —leather jackets lined with corduroy, blue coats of pilot cloth, sou'westers, sea-boots, oilskins. And everywhere was in evidence the economy of space—the narrow bunks, the swinging tables, the incredible lockers. There were the tell-tale compass, the sea-lamps in their gimbals, the blue-backed charts carelessly rolled and tucked away, the signal-flags in alphabetical order, and a mariner's dividers jammed into the woodwork to hold a calendar. At last I was living. Here I sat, inside my first ship, a smuggler, accepted as a comrade by a harpooner and a runaway English sailor who said his name was Scotty.

The first thing that the harpooner, aged nineteen, and the sailor, aged seventeen, did to show that they were men, was to behave like men. The harpooner suggested the eminent desirableness of a drink, and Scotty searched his pockets for dimes and nickels. Then the harpooner carried away a

pink flask to be filled in some blind pig, for there
were no licensed saloons in that locality. We drank
the cheap rotgut out of tumblers. Was I any the
less strong, any the less valiant, than the harpooner and the sailor? They were men. They
proved it by the way they drank. Drink was the
badge of manhood. So I drank with them, drink
by drink, raw and straight, though the damned
stuff could n't compare with a stick of chewing
taffy or a delectable "cannonball." I shuddered
and swallowed my gorge with every drink, though
I manfully hid all such symptoms.

Divers times we filled the flask that afternoon.
All I had was twenty cents, but I put it up like a
man, though with secret regret at the enormous
store of candy it could have bought. The liquor
mounted in the heads of all of us, and the talk of
Scotty and the harpooner was upon running the
Easting down, gales off the Horn and pamperos
off the Plate, lower topsail breezes, southerly bust-
ers, North Pacific gales, and of smashed whale-
boats in the Arctic ice.

"You can't swim in that ice water," said the
harpooner confidentially to me. "You double up
in a minute and go down. When a whale smashes
your boat, the thing to do is to get your belly
across an oar, so that when the cold doubles you
you 'll float."

"Sure," I said, with a grateful nod and an air of
certitude that I, too, would hunt whales and be in
smashed boats in the Arctic Ocean. And, truly, I
registered his advice as singularly valuable infor-
mation, and filed it away in my brain, where it
persists to this day.

But I could n't talk—at first. Heavens! I was
only fourteen, and had never been on the ocean
in my life. I could only listen to the two sea-dogs,
and show my manhood by drinking with them,
fairly and squarely, drink and drink.

The liquor worked its will with me; the talk of Scotty and the harpooner poured through the pent space of the *Idler's* cabin and through my brain like great gusts of wide, free wind; and in imagination I lived my years to come and rocked over the wild, mad, glorious world on multitudinous adventures.

We unbent. Our inhibitions and taciturnities vanished. We were as if we had known each other for years and years, and we pledged ourselves to years of future voyagings together. The harpooner told of misadventures and secret shames. Scotty wept over his poor old mother in Edinburg—a lady, he insisted, gently born—who was in reduced circumstances, who had pinched herself to pay the lump sum to the shipowners for his apprenticeship, whose sacrificing dream had been to see him a merchantman officer and a gentleman, and who was heartbroken because he had deserted his ship in Australia and joined another as a common sailor before the mast. And Scotty proved it. He drew her last sad letter from his pocket and wept over it as he read it aloud. The harpooner and I wept with him, and swore that all three of us would ship on the whaleship *Bonanza*, win a big pay-day, and, still together, make a pilgrimage to Edinburg and lay our store of money in the dear lady's lap.

And, as John Barleycorn heated his way into my brain, thawing my reticence, melting my modesty, talking through me and with me and as me, my adopted twin brother and *alter ego*, I, too, raised my voice to show myself a man and an adventurer, and bragged in detail and at length of how I had crossed San Francisco Bay in my open skiff in a roaring southwester when even the schooner sailors doubted my exploit. Further, I—or John Barleycorn, for it was the same thing—told Scotty that he might be a deep sea sailor and know the last rope on the great deep sea ships, but that when it came to small-boat sailing I could beat him hands down and sail circles around him.

The best of it was that my assertion and brag were true. With reticence and modesty present, I could never have dared tell Scotty my small-boat estimate of him. But it is ever the way of John Barleycorn to loosen the tongue and babble the secret thought.

Scotty, or John Barleycorn, or the pair, was very naturally offended by my remarks. Nor was I loath. I could whip any runaway sailor seventeen years old. Scotty and I flared and raged like young cockerels, until the harpooner poured another round of drinks to enable us to forgive and make up. Which we did, arms around each other's necks, protesting vows of eternal friendship—just like Black Matt and Tom Morrisey, I remembered, in the ranch kitchen in San Mateo. And remembering, I knew that I was at last a man—despite my meager fourteen years—a man as big and manly as those two strapping giants who had quarreled and made up on that memorable Sunday morning of long ago.

By this time the singing stage was reached, and I joined Scotty and the harpooner in snatches of sea songs and chanties. It was here, in the cabin of the *Idler*, that I first heard "Blow the Man Down," "Flying Cloud," and "Whisky, Johnny, Whisky." Oh, it was brave. I was beginning to grasp the meaning of life. Here was no commonplace, no Oakland Estuary, no weary round of throwing newspapers at front doors, delivering ice, and setting up ninepins. All the world was mine, all its paths were under my feet, and John Barleycorn, tricking my fancy, enabled me to anticipate the life of adventure for which I yearned.

We were not ordinary. We were three tipsy young gods, incredibly wise, gloriously genial, and without limit to our powers. Ah!—and I say it now, after the years—could John Barleycorn keep one at such a height, I should never draw a sober breath again. But this is not a world of free freights. One pays according to an iron schedule—for every strength the balanced weakness; for every high a corresponding low; for every fictitious god-like moment an equivalent time in reptilian slime. For every feat of telescoping long days and weeks of life into mad, magnificent instants, one must pay with shortened life, and, oft-times, with savage usury added.

Intenseness and duration are as ancient enemies as fire and water. They are mutually destructive. They cannot co-exist. And John Barleycorn, mighty necromancer though he be, is as much a slave to organic chemistry as we mortals are. We pay for every nerve Marathon we run, nor can John Barleycorn intercede and fend off the just payment. He can lead us to the heights, but he cannot keep us there, else would we all be devotees. And there is no devotee but pays for the mad dances John Barleycorn pipes.

Yet the foregoing is all in after-wisdom spoken. It was no part of the knowledge of the lad, fourteen years old, who sat in the _Idler's_ cabin between the harpooner and the sailor, the air rich in his nostrils with the musty smell of men's sea-gear, roaring in chorus: "Yankee ship come down de ribber—Pull, my bully boys, pull!"

We grew maudlin, and all talked and shouted at once. I had a splendid constitution, a stomach that would digest scrap-iron, and I was still running my Marathon in full vigor when Scotty began to fail and fade. His talk grew incoherent. He groped for words and could not find them, while the ones he found his lips were unable to form. His poisoned consciousness was leaving him. The brightness went out of his eyes, and he looked as stupid as were his efforts to talk. His face and body sagged as his consciousness sagged. (A man cannot sit upright save by an act of will). Scotty's reeling brain could not control his muscles. All his correlations were breaking down. He strove to take another drink, and feebly dropped the tumbler on the floor. Then, to my amazement, weeping bitterly, he rolled into a bunk on his back and immediately snored off to sleep.

The harpooner and I drank on, grinning in a superior way to each other over Scotty's plight. The last flask was opened, and we drank it between us, to the accompaniment of Scotty's stertorous breathing. Then the harpooner faded away into his bunk, and I was left alone, unthrown, on the field of battle.

I was very proud, and John Barleycorn was proud with me. I could carry my drink. I was a man. I had drunk two men, drink for drink, into unconsciousness. And I was still on my two feet, upright, making my way on deck to get air into my scorching lungs. It was in this bout on the *Idler* that I discovered what a good stomach and a strong head I had for drink—a bit of knowledge that was to be a source of pride in succeeding years, and that ultimately I was to come to consider a great affliction. The fortunate man is the one who cannot take more than a couple of drinks without becoming intoxicated. The unfortunate wight is the one who can take many glasses without betraying a sign; who *must* take numerous glasses in order to get the "kick."

The sun was setting when I came on the *Idler's* deck. There were plenty of bunks below. I did not need to go home. But I wanted to demonstrate to myself how much I was a man. There lay my skiff astern. The last of a strong ebb was running out in channel in the teeth of an ocean breeze of forty miles an hour. I could see the stiff whitecaps, and the suck and run of the current was plainly visible in the face and trough of each one.

I set sail, cast off, took my place at the tiller, the sheet in my hand, and headed across channel. The skiff heeled over and plunged into it madly. The spray began to fly. I was at the pinnacle of exaltation. I sang "Blow the Man Down" as I sailed. I was no boy of fourteen, living the mediocre ways of the sleepy town called Oakland. I was a man, a god, and the very elements rendered me allegiance as I bitted them to my will.

The tide was out. A full hundred yards of soft mud intervened between the boat wharf and the water. I pulled up my centerboard, ran full tilt into the mud, took in sail, and, standing in the stern as I had often done at a low tide, I began to shove the skiff with an oar. It was then that my correlations began to break down. I lost my balance and pitched headforemost into the ooze. Then, and for the first time, as I floundered to my feet covered with slime, the blood running down my arms from a scrape against a barnacled stake, I knew that I was drunk. But what of it? Across the channel two strong sailormen lay unconscious in their bunks where I had drunk them. I *was* a man. I was still on my legs, if they *were* knee deep in mud. I disdained to get back into the skiff. I waded through the mud, shoving the skiff before me and yammering the chant of my manhood to the world.

I paid for it. I was sick for a couple of days, meanly sick, and my arms were painfully poisoned from the barnacle scratches. For a week I could not use them, and it was a torture to put on and take off my clothes.

I swore, "Never again!" The game wasn't worth it. The price was too stiff. I had no moral qualms. My revulsion was purely physical. No exalted moments were worth such hours of misery and wretchedness. When I got back to my skiff, I shunned the *Idler*. I would cross the opposite side of the channel to go around her. Scotty had disappeared. The harpooner was still about, but him I avoided. Once, when he landed on the boat-wharf, I hid in a shed so as to escape seeing him. I was afraid he would propose some more drinking, maybe have a flask full of whisky in his pocket.

And yet—and here enters the necromancy of John Barleycorn—that afternoon's drunk on the *Idler* had been a purple passage flung into the monotony of my days. It was memorable. My mind dwelt on it continually. I went over the details, over and over again. Among other things, I had got into the cogs and springs of men's actions. I had seen Scotty weep about his own worthlessness and the sad case of his Edinburg mother who was a lady. The harpooner had told me terribly wonderful things of himself. I had caught a myriad enticing and inflammatory hints of a world beyond my world, and for which I was certainly as fitted as the two lads who had drunk with me. I had got behind men's souls. I had got behind my own soul and found unguessed potencies and greatnesses.

Yes, that day stood out above all my other days. To this day it so stands out. The memory of it is branded in my brain. But the price exacted was too high. I refused to play and pay, and returned to my cannonballs and taffy-slabs. The point is that all the chemistry of my healthy, normal body drove me away from alcohol. The stuff did n't agree with me. It was abominable. But despite this, circumstance was to continue to drive me toward John Barleycorn, to drive me again and again, until, after long years, the time should come when I would look up John Barleycorn in every haunt of men—look him up and hail him gladly as benefactor and friend. And detest and hate him all the time. Yes, he is a strange friend, John Barleycorn.

Chapter VII

I WAS barely turned fifteen, and working long hours in a cannery. Month in and month out, the shortest day I ever worked was ten hours. When to ten hours of actual work at a machine is added the noon hour; the walking to work and walking home from work; the getting up in the morning, dressing, and eating; the eating at night, undressing, and going to bed, there remains no more than the nine hours out of the twenty-four required by a healthy youngster for sleep. Out of those nine hours, after I was in bed and ere my eyes drowsed shut, I managed to steal a little time for reading.

But many a night I did not knock off work until midnight. On occasion I worked eighteen and twenty hours on a stretch. Once I worked at my machine for thirty-six consecutive hours. And there were weeks on end when I never knocked off work earlier than eleven o'clock, got home and in bed at half after midnight, and was called at half-past five to dress, eat, walk to work, and be at my machine at seven o'clock whistle blow.

No moments here to be stolen for my beloved books. And what had John Barleycorn to do with so strenuous, Stoic toil of a lad just turned fifteen? He had everything to do with it. Let me show you. I asked myself if this were the meaning of life—to be a work-beast? I knew of no horse in the city of Oakland that worked the hours I worked.

If this were living, I was entirely unenamored of it. I remembered my skiff, lying idle and accumulating barnacles at the boat-wharf; I remembered the wind that blew every day on the bay, the sunrises and sunsets I never saw; the bite of the salt air in my nostrils, the bite of the salt water on my flesh when I plunged overside; I remembered all the beauty and the wonder and the sense-delights of the world denied me. There was only one way to escape my deadening toil. I must get out and away on the water. I must earn my bread on the water. And the way of the water led inevitably to John Barleycorn. I did not know this. And when I did learn it, I was courageous enough not to retreat back to my bestial life at the machine.

I wanted to be where the winds of adventure blew. And the winds of adventure blew the oyster pirate sloops up and down San Francisco Bay, from raided oyster-beds and fights at night on shoal and flat, to markets in the morning against city wharves, where peddlers and saloon-keepers came down to buy. Every raid on an oyster-bed was a felony. The penalty was state imprisonment, the stripes and the lockstep. And what of that? The men in stripes worked a shorter day than I at my machine. And there was vastly more romance in being an oyster pirate or a convict than in being a machine slave. And behind it all, behind all of me with youth a-bubble, whispered Romance, Adventure.

So I interviewed my Mammy Jennie, my old nurse at whose black breast I had suckled. She was more prosperous than my folks. She was nursing sick people at a good weekly wage. Would she lend her "white child" the money? *Would she?* What she had was mine.

Then I sought out French Frank, the oyster pirate, who wanted to sell, I had heard, his sloop, the *Razzle Dazzle*. I found him lying at anchor on the Alameda side of the estuary, near the Webster Street bridge, with visitors aboard, whom he was entertaining with afternoon wine. He came on deck to talk business. He was willing to sell. But it was Sunday. Besides, he had guests. On the morrow he would make out the bill of sale and I could enter into possession. And in the meantime I must come below and meet his friends. They were two sisters, Mamie and Tess; a Mrs. Hadley, who chaperoned them; "Whisky" Bob, a youthful oyster pirate of sixteen; and "Spider" Healey, a black-whiskered wharf-rat of twenty. Mamie, who was Spider's niece, was called the Queen of the Oyster Pirates, and, on occasion, presided at their revels. French Frank was in love with her, though I did not know it at the time; and she steadfastly refused to marry him.

French Frank poured a tumbler of red wine from a big demijohn to drink to our transaction. I remembered the red wine of the Italian rancho, and shuddered inwardly. Whisky and beer were not quite so repulsive. But the Queen of the Oyster Pirates was looking at me, a part-emptied glass in her own hand. I had my pride. If I was only fifteen, at least I could not show myself any less a man than she. Besides, there were her sister, and Mrs. Hadley, and the young oyster pirate, and the whiskered wharf-rat, all with glasses in their hands. Was I a milk and water sop? No; a thousand times no, and a thousand glasses no. I downed the tumblerful like a man.

French Frank was elated by the sale, which I had bound with a twenty-dollar goldpiece. He poured more wine. I had learned my strong head and stomach, and I was certain I could drink with them in a temperate way and not poison myself for a week to come. I could stand as much as they; and besides, they had already been drinking for some time.

We got to singing. Spider sang "The Boston Burglar" and "Black Lulu." The Queen sang "Then I Wisht I were a Little Bird." And her sister Tess sang "Oh, Treat My Daughter Kind-i-ly." The fun grew fast and furious. I found myself able to miss drinks without being noticed or called to account. Also, standing in the companionway, head and shoulders out and glass in hand, I could fling the wine overboard.

I reasoned something like this: It is a queerness of these people that they like this vile-tasting wine. Well, let them. I cannot quarrel with their tastes. My manhood, according to their queer notions, must compel me to appear to like this wine. Very well. I shall so appear. But I shall drink no more than is unavoidable.

And the Queen began to make love to me, the latest recruit to the oyster pirate fleet, and no mere hand, but a master and owner. She went upon deck to take the air, and took me with her. She knew, of course, but I never dreamed, how French Frank was raging down below. Then Tess joined us, sitting on the cabin; and Spider, and Bob; and at the last, Mrs. Hadley and French Frank. And we sat there, glasses in hand, and sang, while the big demijohn went around; and I was the only strictly sober one.

And I enjoyed it as no one of them was able to enjoy it. Here, in this atmosphere of bohemianism, I could not but contrast the scene with my scene of the day before, sitting at my machine, in the stifling, shut-in air, repeating, endlessly repeating, at top speed, my series of mechanical motions. And here I sat now, glass in hand, in warm-glowing camaraderie, with the oyster pirates, adventurers who refused to be slaves to petty routine, who flouted restrictions and the law, who carried their lives and their liberty in their hands. And it was through John Barleycorn

that I came to join this glorious company of free
souls, unashamed and unafraid.

And the afternoon sea breeze blew its tang into
my lungs, and curled the waves in mid-channel.
Before it came the scow schooners, wing-and-wing,
blowing their horns for the drawbridges to open.
Red-stacked tugs tore by, rocking the *Razzle Dazzle*
in the waves of their wake. A sugar bark towed
from the "boneyard" to sea. The sun-wash was
on the crisping water, and life was big. And Spider sang:

> "Oh, it 's Lulu, black Lulu, my darling,
>   Oh, it 's where have you been so long?
> Been layin' in jail,
> A-waitin' for bail,
>   Till my bully comes rollin' along."

There it was, the smack and slap of the spirit of
revolt, of adventure, of romance, of the things
forbidden and done defiantly and grandly. And I
knew that on the morrow I would not go back to
my machine at the cannery. To-morrow I would
be an oyster pirate, as free a freebooter as the
century and the waters of San Francisco Bay would
permit. Spider had already agreed to sail with me
as my crew of one, and, also, as cook while I did
the deck work. We would outfit our grub and
water in the morning, hoist the big mainsail (which
was a bigger piece of canvas than any I had ever
sailed under), and beat our way out the estuary
on the first of the sea breeze and the last of the
ebb. Then we would slack sheets, and on the first
of the flood run down the bay to the Asparagus
Islands, where we would anchor miles off shore.
And at last my dream would be realized: I would
sleep upon the water. And next morning I would
wake upon the water; and thereafter all my days
and nights would be on the water.

And the Queen asked me to row her ashore in my skiff, when at sunset French Frank prepared to take his guests ashore. Nor did I catch the significance of his abrupt change of plan when he turned the task of rowing his skiff over to Whisky Bob, himself remaining on board the sloop. Nor did I understand Spider's grinning side-remark to me: "Gee! There's nothin' slow about *you*." How could it possibly enter my boy's head that a grizzled man of fifty should be jealous of me?

Chapter VIII

WE MET by appointment, early Monday morning, to complete the deal, in Johnny Heinhold's "Last Chance"—a saloon, of course, for the transactions of men. I paid the money over, received the bill of sale, and French Frank treated. This struck me as an evident custom, and a logical one—the seller, who receives the money, to wet a piece of it in the establishment where the trade was consummated. But to my surprise, French Frank treated the house. He and I drank, which seemed just; but why should Johnny Heinhold, who owned the saloon and waited behind the bar, be invited to drink? I figured it immediately that he made a profit on the very drink he drank. I could, in a way, considering that they were friends and shipmates, understand Spider and Whisky Bob being asked to drink; but why should the longshoremen, Bill Kelly and Soup Kennedy, be asked?

Then there was Pat, the Queen's brother, making a total of eight of us. It was early morning and all ordered whisky. What could I do, here in this company of big men, all drinking whisky? "Whisky," I said, with the careless air of one who had said it a thousand times. And such whisky! I tossed it down. A-r-r-r-gh! I can taste it yet.

And I was appalled at the price French Frank had paid—eighty cents. *Eighty cents!* It was an outrage to my thrifty soul. Eighty cents—the equivalent of eight long hours of my toil at the machine, gone down our throats and gone like that, in a twinkling, leaving only a bad taste in my mouth. There was no discussion but that French Frank was a waster.

I was anxious to be gone, out into the sunshine, out over the water to my glorious boat. But all hands lingered. Even Spider, my crew, lingered. No hint broke through my obtuseness of why they lingered. I have often thought since of how they must have regarded me, the newcomer being welcomed into their company, standing at bar with them, and not standing for a single round of drinks.

French Frank, who, unknown to me, had swallowed his chagrin since the day before, now that the money for the *Razzle Dazzle* was in his pocket began to behave curiously toward me. I sensed the change in his attitude, saw the forbidding glitter in his eyes, and wondered. The more I saw of men, the queerer they became. Johnny Heinhold leaned across the bar and whispered in my ear: "He's got it in for you. Watch out."

I nodded comprehension of his statement, and acquiescence in it, as a man should nod who knows all about men. But secretly I was perplexed. Heavens! How was I, who had worked hard and read books of adventure, and who was only fifteen years old, who had not dreamed of giving the Queen of the Oyster Pirates a second thought, and who did not know that French Frank was madly and Latinly in love with her—how was I to guess that I had done him shame? And how was I to guess that the story of how the Queen had thrown him down on his own boat, the moment I hove in sight, was already the gleeful gossip of the waterfront? And by the same token, how was I to guess that her brother Pat's offishness with me was anything else than temperamental gloominess of spirit?

Whisky Bob got me aside a moment. "Keep your eyes open," he muttered. "Take my tip. French Frank's ugly. I 'm going up river with him to get a schooner for oystering. When he gets down on the beds, watch out. He says he 'll run you down. After dark, any time he 's around, change your anchorage and douse your riding light. Savve?"

Oh, certainly, I savve'd. I nodded my head, and as one man to another thanked him for his tip; and drifted back to the group at the bar. No; I did not treat. I never dreamed that I was expected to treat. I left with Spider, and my ears burn now as I try to surmise the things they must have said about me.

I asked Spider, in an off-hand way, what was eating French Frank. "He 's crazy jealous of you," was the answer. "Do you think so?" I stalled, and dismissed the matter as not worth thinking about.

But I leave it to any one—the swell of my fifteen-years-old manhood at learning that French Frank, the adventurer of fifty, the sailor of all the seas of all the world, was jealous of me—and jealous over a girl most romantically named the Queen of the Oyster Pirates. I had read of such things in books, and regarded them as personal probabilities of a distant maturity. Oh, I felt a rare young devil, as we hoisted the big mainsail that morning, broke out anchor, and filled away close-hauled on the three-mile beat to windward out into the bay.

Such was my escape from the killing machine-toil, and my introduction to the oyster pirates. True, the introduction had begun with drink, and the life promised to continue with drink. But was I to stay away from it for such reason? Wherever life ran free and great, there men drank. Romance and adventure seemed always to go down the street locked arm in arm with John Barleycorn. To know the two, I must know the third. Or else I must go back to my free-library books and read of the deeds of other men and do no deeds of my own save slave for ten cents an hour at a machine in a cannery.

No; I was not to be deterred from this brave life on the water by the fact that the water-dwellers had queer and expensive desires for beer and wine and whisky. What if their notions of happiness included the strange one of seeing me drink? When they persisted in buying the stuff and thrusting it upon me, why, I would drink it. It was the price I would pay for their comradeship. And I did n't have to get drunk. I had not got drunk the Sunday afternoon I arranged to buy the *Razzle Dazzle*, despite the fact that none of the rest was sober. Well, I could go on into the future that way, drinking the stuff when it gave them pleasure that I should drink it, but carefully avoiding over-drinking.

Chapter IX

GRADUAL as was my development as a heavy drinker among the oyster pirates, the real heavy drinking came suddenly and was the result, not of desire for alcohol, but of an intellectual conviction.

The more I saw of the life, the more I was enamored of it. I can never forget my thrills, the first night I took part in a concerted raid, when we assembled on board the *Annie*—rough men, big and unafraid, and weazened wharf rats, some of them ex-convicts, all of them enemies of the law and meriting jail, in sea-boots and sea-gear, talking in gruff, low voices, and "Big" George with revolvers strapped about his waist to show that he meant business.

Oh, I know, looking back, that the whole thing was sordid and silly. But I was not looking back in those days when I was rubbing shoulders with John Barleycorn and beginning to accept him. The life was brave and wild, and I was living the adventure I had read so much about.

Nelson, "Young Scratch" they called him to distinguish him from "Old Scratch," his father, sailed in the sloop *Reindeer*, partners with one "Clam." Clam was a dare-devil, but Nelson was a reckless maniac. He was twenty years old, with the body of a Hercules. When he was shot in Benicia, a couple of years later, the coroner said he was the greatest-shouldered man he had ever seen laid on a slab.

Nelson could not read nor write. He had been "dragged" up by his father on San Francisco Bay, and boats were second nature with him. His strength was prodigious, and his reputation along the waterfront for violence was anything but savory. He had Berserker rages and did mad, terrible things. I made his acquaintance the first cruise of the *Razzle Dazzle*, and saw him sail the *Reindeer* in a blow and dredge oysters all around the rest of us as we lay at two anchors, troubled with fear of going ashore.

He was some man, this Nelson; and when, passing by the Last Chance saloon, he spoke to me, I felt very proud. But try to imagine my pride when he promptly asked me in to have a drink. I stood at bar and drank a glass of beer with him, and talked manfully of oysters, and boats, and of the mystery of who had put the load of buckshot through the *Annie's* mainsail.

We talked and lingered at the bar. It seemed to me strange that we lingered. We had had our beer. But who was I to lead the way outside when great Nelson chose to lean against the bar? After a few minutes, to my surprise, he asked me to have another drink, which I did. And still we talked, and Nelson evinced no intention of leaving the bar.

Bear with me while I explain the way of my reasoning and of my innocence. First of all, I was very proud to be in the company of Nelson, who was the most heroic figure among the oyster pirates and bay adventurers. Unfortunately for my stomach and mucous membranes, Nelson had a strange quirk of nature that made him find happiness in treating me to beer. I had no moral disinclination for beer, and just because I did n't like the taste of it and the weight of it was no reason I should forego the honor of his company. It was his whim to drink beer, and to have me drink beer with him. Very well, I would put up with the passing discomfort.

So we continued to talk at bar, and to drink beer ordered and paid for by Nelson. I think, now, when I look back upon it, that Nelson was curious. He wanted to find out just what kind of a gink I was. He wanted to see how many times I'd let him treat without offering to treat in return.

After I had drunk half-a-dozen glasses, my policy of temperateness in mind, I decided that I had had enough for that time. So I mentioned that I was going aboard the *Razzle Dazzle*, then lying at the city wharf a hundred yards away.

I said good-by to Nelson, and went on down the wharf. But John Barleycorn, to the extent of six glasses, went with me. My brain tingled and was very much alive. I was uplifted by my sense of manhood. I, a truly-true oyster pirate, was going aboard my own boat after hobnobbing in the Last Chance with Nelson, the greatest oyster pirate of us all. Strong in my brain was the vision of us leaning against the bar and drinking beer. And curious it was, I decided, this whim of nature that made men happy in spending good money for beer for a fellow like me who didn't want it.

As I pondered this, I recollected that several times other men, in couples, had entered the Last Chance, and first one, then the other, had treated to drinks. I remembered, on the drunk on the *Idler*, how Scotty and the harpooner and myself had raked and scraped dimes and nickels with which to buy the whisky. Then came my boy code: when on a day a fellow gave another a "cannonball" or a chunk of taffy, on some other day he would expect to receive back a cannonball or a chunk of taffy.

That was why Nelson had lingered at the bar. Having bought a drink, he had waited for me to buy one. *I had let him buy six drinks and never once offered to treat.* And he was the great Nelson! I could feel myself blushing with shame. I sat down on the stringer-piece of the wharf and buried my face in my hands. And the heat of my shame burned up my neck and into my cheeks and forehead. I have blushed many times in my life, but never have I experienced so terrible a blush as that one.

And sitting there on the stringer-piece in my shame, I did a great deal of thinking and transvaluing of values. I had been born poor. Poor I had lived. I had gone hungry on occasion. I had never had toys nor playthings like other children. My first memories of life were pinched by poverty. The pinch of poverty had been chronic. I was eight years old when I wore my first little undershirt actually sold in a store across the counter. And then it had been only one little undershirt. When it was soiled I had to return to the awful home-made things until it was washed. I had been so proud of it that I insisted on wearing it without any outer garment. For the first time I mutinied against my mother—mutinied myself into hysteria, until she let me wear the store undershirt so all the world could see.

Only a man who has undergone famine can properly value food; only sailors and desert-dwellers know the meaning of fresh water. And only a child, with a child's imagination, can come to know the meaning of things it has been long denied. I early discovered that the only things I could have were those I got for myself. My meager childhood developed meagerness. The first things I had been able to get for myself had been cigarette pictures, cigarette posters, and cigarette albums. I had not had the spending of the money I earned, so I traded "extra" newspapers for these treasures. I traded duplicates with the other boys, and circulating, as I did, all about town, I had greater opportunities for trading and acquiring.

It was not long before I had completed every series issued by every cigarette manufacturer—such as the Great Race Horses, Parisian Beauties, Women of All Nations, Flags of All Nations, Noted Actors, Champion Prize Fighters, etc. And each series I had three different ways: in the card from the cigarette package, in the poster, and in the album.

Then I began to accumulate duplicate sets, duplicate albums. I traded for other things that boys valued and which they usually bought with money given them by their parents. Naturally, they did not have the keen sense of values that I had, who was never given money to buy anything. I traded for postage stamps, for minerals, for curios, for birds' eggs, for marbles (I had a more magnificent collection of agates than I have ever seen any other boy possess—and the nucleus of the collection was a handful worth at least three dollars which I had kept as security for twenty cents I loaned to a messenger-boy who was sent to reform school before he could redeem them).

I'd trade anything and everything for anything else, and turn it over in a dozen more trades until it was transmuted into something that was worth something. I was famous as a trader. I was notorious as a miser. I could even make a junk man weep when I had dealings with him. Other boys called me in to sell for them their collections of bottles, rags, old iron, grain and gunny sacks, and five-gallon oil-cans—ay, and gave me a commission for doing it.

And this was the thrifty, close-fisted boy, accustomed to slave at a machine for ten cents an hour, who sat on the stringer-piece and considered the matter of beer at five cents a glass and gone in a moment with nothing to show for it. I was now with men I admired. I was proud to be with them. Had all my pinching and saving brought me the equivalent of one of the many thrills which had been mine since I came among the oyster pirates? Then what was worth while—money or thrills? These men had no horror of squandering a nickel, or many nickels. They were magnificently careless of money, calling up eight men to drink whisky at ten cents a glass, as French Frank had done. Why, Nelson had just spent sixty cents on beer for the two of us.

Which was it to be? I was aware that I was making a grave decision. I was deciding between money and men, between niggardliness and romance. Either I must throw overboard all my old values of money and look upon it as something to be flung about wastefully, or I must throw overboard my comradeship with those men whose peculiar quirks made them care for strong drink.

I retraced my steps up the wharf to the Last Chance where Nelson still stood outside. "Come on and have a beer," I invited. Again we stood at bar and drank and talked, but this time it was I who paid—ten cents! A whole hour of my labor at a machine for a drink of something I did n't want and which tasted rotten. But it was n't difficult. I had achieved a concept. Money no longer counted. It was comradeship that counted. "Have another," I said. And we had another, and I paid for it. Nelson, with the wisdom of the skilled drinker, said to the barkeeper, "Make mine a small one, Johnny." Johnny nodded and gave him a glass that contained only a third as much as the glasses we had been drinking. Yet the charge was the same—five cents.

By this time I was getting nicely jingled, so such extravagance did n't hurt me much. Besides, I was learning. There was more in this buying of drinks than mere quantity. I got my finger on it.

There was a stage when the beer did n't count at all, but just the spirit of comradeship of drinking together. And, ha!—another thing! I, too, could call for small beers and minimize by two-thirds the detestable freightage with which comradeship burdened one.

"I had to go aboard to get some money," I remarked casually, as we drank, in the hope Nelson would take it as an explanation of why I had let him treat six consecutive times.

"Oh, well, you did n't have to do that," he answered. "Johnny 'll trust a fellow like you—won't you, Johnny?"

"Sure," Johnny agreed, with a smile.

"How much you got down against me?" Nelson queried.

Johnny pulled out the book he kept behind the bar, found Nelson's page, and added up the account of several dollars. At once I became possessed with a desire to have a page in that book. Almost it seemed the final badge of manhood.

After a couple more drinks, for which I insisted on paying, Nelson decided to go. We parted true comradely, and I wandered down the wharf to the *Razzle Dazzle*. Spider was just building the fire for supper.

"Where 'd you get it?" he grinned up at me through the open companion.

"Oh, I 've been with Nelson," I said carelessly, trying to hide my pride.

Then an idea came to me. Here was another one of them. Now that I had achieved my concept, I might as well practice it thoroughly. "Come on," I said, "up to Johnny's and have a drink."

Going up the wharf, we met Clam coming down. Clam was Nelson's partner, and he was a fine, brave, handsome, mustached man of thirty—everything, in short, that his nickname did not connote. "Come on," I said, "and have a drink." He came. As we turned into the Last Chance, there was Pat, the Queen's brother, coming out.

"What's your hurry?" I greeted him. "We're having a drink. Come on along." "I've just had one," he demurred. "What of it?—we're having one now," I retorted. And Pat consented to join us, and I melted my way into his good graces with a couple of glasses of beer. Oh! I was learning things that afternoon about John Barleycorn. There was more in him than the bad taste when you swallowed him. Here, at the absurd cost of ten cents, a gloomy, grouchy individual, who threatened to become an enemy, was made into a good friend, even genial, his looks were kindly, and our voices mellowed together as we talked water-front and oyster-bed gossip.

"Small beer for me, Johnny," I said, when the others had ordered schooners. Yet I said it like the accustomed drinker, carelessly, casually, as a sort of spontaneous thought that had just occurred to me. Looking back, I am confident that the only one there who guessed I was a tyro at bar-drinking was Johnny Heinhold.

"Where'd he get it?" I overheard Spider confidentially ask Johnny.

"Oh, he's been sousin' here with Nelson all afternoon," was Johnny's answer.

I never let on that I'd heard, but *proud?* Ay, even the barkeeper was giving me commendation as a man. *"He's been sousin' here with Nelson all afternoon."* Magic words! The accolade delivered by a barkeeper with a beer glass!

I remembered that French Frank had treated Johnny the day I bought the *Razzle Dazzle*. The glasses were filled, and we were ready to drink. "Have something yourself, Johnny," I said, with an air of having intended to say it all the time but of having been a trifle remiss because of the interesting conversation I had been holding with Clam and Pat.

Johnny looked at me with quick sharpness, divining, I am positive, the strides I was making in my education, and poured himself whisky from his private bottle. This hit me for a moment on my thrifty side. He had taken a ten-cent drink when the rest of us were drinking five-cent drinks! But the hurt was only for a moment. I dismissed it as ignoble, remembered my concept, and did not give myself away.

"You 'd better put me down in the book for this," I said, when we had finished the drink. And I had the satisfaction of seeing a fresh page devoted to my name and a charge penciled for a round of drinks amounting to thirty cents. And I glimpsed, as through a golden haze, a future wherein that page would be much-charged, and crossed off, and charged again.

I treated a second time around, and then, to my amazement, Johnny redeemed himself in that matter of the ten-cent drink. He treated us a round from behind the bar, and I decided that he had arithmetically evened things up handsomely.

"Let 's go around to the St. Louis House," Spider suggested, when we got outside. Pat, who had been shoveling coal all day, had gone home, and Clam had gone upon the *Reindeer* to cook supper.

So around Spider and I went to the St. Louis House—my first visit—a huge barroom, where perhaps fifty men, mostly longshoremen, were congregated. And there I met Stew Kennedy for the second time, and Bill Kelly. And Smith, of the *Annie*, drifted in—he of the belt-buckled revolvers. And Nelson showed up. And I met others, including the Vigy brothers, who ran the place, and, chiefest of all, Joe Goose, with the wicked eyes, the twisted nose, and the flowered vest, who played the harmonica like a roystering angel and went on the most atrocious tears that even the Oakland water-front could conceive of and admire.

As I bought drinks—others treated as well—the thought flickered across my mind that Mammy Jennie was n't going to be repaid much on her loan out of that week's earnings of the *Razzle Dazzle*. "But what of it?" I thought, or rather, John Barleycorn thought it for me. "You 're a man and you 're getting acquainted with men. Mammy Jennie does n't need the money as promptly as all that. She is n't starving. You know that. She 's got other money in bank. Let her wait, and pay her back gradually."

And thus it was I learned another trait of John Barleycorn. He inhibits morality. Wrong conduct that it is impossible for one to do sober, is done quite easily when one is not sober. In fact, it is the only thing one can do, for John Barleycorn's inhibition rises like a wall between one's immediate desires and long-learned morality.

I dismissed my thought of debt to Mammy Jennie and proceeded to get acquainted at the trifling expense of some trifling money and a jingle that was growing unpleasant. Who took me on board and put me to bed that night I do not know, but I imagine it must have been Spider.

Chapter X

AND SO I won my manhood's spurs. My status on the water-front and with the oyster pirates became immediately excellent. I was looked upon as a good fellow, as well as no coward. And somehow, from the day I achieved that concept sitting on the stringer piece of the Oakland City Wharf, I have never cared much for money. No one has ever considered me a miser since, while my carelessness of money is a source of anxiety and worry to some that know me.

So completely did I break with my parsimonious past that I sent word home to my mother to call in the boys of the neighborhood and give to them all my collections. I never even cared to learn what boys got what collections. I was a man, now, and I made a clean sweep of everything that bound me to my boyhood.

My reputation grew. When the story went around the water-front of how French Frank had tried to run me down with his schooner, and of how I had stood on the deck of the *Razzle Dazzle*, a cocked double-barreled shotgun in my hands, steering with my feet and holding her to her course and compelled him to put up his wheel and keep away, the water-front decided that there was something to me despite my youth. And I continued to show what was in me. There were the times I brought the *Razzle Dazzle* in with a bigger load of oysters than any other two-man craft; there was

the time when we raided far down in Lower Bay
and mine was the only craft back at daylight to
the anchorage off Asparagus Island; there was the
Thursday night we raced for market and I brought
the *Razzle Dazzle* in without a rudder, first of the
fleet, and skimmed the cream of the Friday morning trade; and there was the time I brought her in
from Upper Bay under a jib, when Scotty burned
my mainsail. (Yes; it was Scotty of the *Idler* adventure. Irish had followed Spider on board the *Razzle
Dazzle*, and Scotty, turning up, had taken Irish's
place).

But the things I did on the water only partly
counted. What completed everything and won for
me the title of "Prince of the Oyster Beds," was
that I was a good fellow ashore with my money,
buying drinks like a man. I little dreamed that the
time would come when the Oakland water-front,
which had shocked me at first, would be shocked
and annoyed by the deviltry of the things I did.

But always the life was tied up with drinking.
The saloons are poor men's clubs. Saloons are
congregating places. We engaged to meet one another in saloons. We celebrated our good fortune
or wept our grief in saloons. We got acquainted in
saloons.

Can I ever forget the afternoon I met "Old
Scratch," Nelson's father? It was in the Last
Chance. Johnny Heinhold introduced us. That Old
Scratch was Nelson's father was noteworthy enough.
But there was more to it than that. He was owner
and master of the scow-schooner *Annie Mine*, and
some day I might ship as a sailor with him. Still
more, he was romance. He was a blue-eyed,
yellow-haired, raw-boned Viking, big-bodied and
strong-muscled despite his age. And he had sailed
the seas in ships of all nations in the old savage
sailing days.

I had heard many weird tales about him, and

worshiped him from a distance. It took the saloon
to bring us together. Even so, our acquaintance
might have been no more than a handgrip and a
word—he was a laconic old fellow—had it not
been for the drinking.

"Have a drink," I said, with promptitude, after
the pause which I had learned good form in drinking dictates. Of course, while we drank our beer,
which I had paid for, it was incumbent on him to
listen to me and to talk to me. And Johnny, like a
true host, made the tactful remarks that enabled
us to find mutual topics of conversation. And of
course, having drunk my beer, Captain Nelson
must now buy beer in turn. This led to more
talking, and Johnny drifted out of the conversation to wait on other customers.

The more beer Captain Nelson and I drank the
better we got acquainted. In me he found an ap-
preciative listener, who, by virtue of book-reading,
knew much about the sea-life he had lived. So he
drifted back to his wild young days, and spun
many a rare yarn for me, while we downed beer,
treat by treat, all through a blessed summer afternoon. And it was only John Barleycorn that made
possible that long afternoon with the old sea dog.

It was Johnny Heinhold who secretly warned
me across the bar that I was getting pickled and
advised me to take small beers. But as long as
Captain Nelson drank large beers, my pride for-
bade anything else than large beers. And not until
the skipper ordered his first small beer did I order
one for myself. Oh, when we came to a lingering
fond farewell, I was drunk. But I had the satisfaction of seeing Old Scratch as drunk as I. My
youthful modesty scarcely let me dare believe that
the hardened old bucaneer was even drunker.

And afterwards, from Spider, and Pat, and Clam,
and Johnny Heinhold, and others, came the tips
that Old Scratch liked me and had nothing but

good words for the fine lad I was. Which was the more remarkable, because he was known as a savage, cantankerous old cuss who never liked anybody. (His very nickname, "Scratch," arose from a Berserker trick of his, in fighting, of tearing off his opponent's face). And that I had won to his friendship, all thanks were due to John Barleycorn. I have given the incident merely as an example of the multitudinous lures and draws and services by which John Barleycorn wins his followers.

Chapter XI

A ND STILL there arose in me no desire for alcohol, no chemical demand. In years and years of heavy drinking, drinking did not beget the desire. Drinking was the way of the life I led, the way of the men with whom I lived. While away on my cruises on the bay, I took no drink along; and while out on the bay the thought of the desirableness of a drink never crossed my mind. It was not until I tied the *Razzle Dazzle* up to the wharf and got ashore in the congregating places of men, where drink flowed, that the buying of drinks for other men, and the accepting of drinks from other men, devolved upon me as a social duty and a manhood rite.

Then, too, there were the times, lying at the city wharf or across the estuary on the sandpit, when the Queen, and her sister, and her brother Pat, and Mrs. Hadley came aboard. It was my boat. I was host, and I could only dispense hospitality in the terms of their understanding of it. So I would rush Spider, or Irish, or Scotty, or whoever was my crew, with the can for beer and the demijohn for red wine. And again, lying at the wharf disposing of my oysters, there were dusky twilights when big policemen and plain clothes men stole on board. And because we lived in the shadow of the police, we opened oysters and fed them to them with squirts of pepper sauce, and rushed the growler or got stronger stuff in bottles.

Drink as I would, I could n't come to like John Barleycorn. I valued him extremely well for his associations, but not for the taste of him. All the time I was striving to be a man amongst men, and all the time I nursed secret and shameful desires for candy. But I would have died before I 'd let anybody guess it. I used to indulge in lonely debauches, on nights when I knew my crew was going to sleep ashore. I would go up to the Free Library, exchange my books, buy a quarter's worth of all sorts of candy that chewed and lasted, sneak aboard the *Razzle Dazzle*, lock myself in the cabin, go to bed, and lie there long hours of bliss, reading and chewing candy. And those were the only times I felt that I got my real money's worth. Dollars and dollars, across the bar, could n't buy the satisfaction that twenty-five cents did in a candy store. As my drinking grew heavier, I began to note more and more that it was in the drinking bouts the purple passages occurred. Drunks were always memorable. At such times things happened. Men like Joe Goose dated existence from drunk to drunk. The longshoremen all looked forward to their Saturday night drunk. We of the oyster boats waited until we had disposed of our cargoes before we got really started, though a scattering of drinks and a meeting of a chance friend sometimes precipitated an accidental drunk.

In ways, the accidental drunks were the best. Stranger and more exciting things happened at such times. As, for instance, the Sunday when Nelson and French Frank and Captain Spink stole the stolen salmon boat from Whisky Bob and Nicky the Greek. Changes had taken place in the personnel of the oyster boats. Nelson had got into a fight with Bill Kelly on the *Annie* and was carrying a bullet-hole through his left hand. Also, having quarreled with Clam and broken partnership, Nelson had sailed the *Reindeer*, his arm in a sling, with a crew of two deep-water sailors, and he had sailed so madly as to frighten them ashore. Such was the tale of his recklessness they spread, that no one on the water-front would go out with Nelson. So the *Reindeer*, crewless, lay across the estuary at the sandpit. Beside her lay the *Razzle Dazzle* with a burned mainsail and with Scotty and me on board. Whisky Bob had fallen out with French Frank and gone on a raid "up river" with Nicky the Greek.

The result of this raid was a brand new Columbia River salmon boat, stolen from an Italian fisherman. We oyster pirates were all visited by the searching Italian, and we were convinced, from what we knew of their movements, that Whisky Bob and Nicky the Greek were the guilty parties. But where was the salmon boat? Hundreds of Greek and Italian fishermen, up river and down bay, had searched every slough and tule patch for it. When the owner despairingly offered a reward of fifty dollars, our interest increased and the mystery deepened.

One Sunday morning, old Captain Spink paid me a visit. The conversation was confidential. He had just been fishing in his skiff in the old Alameda ferry slip. As the tide went down, he had noticed a rope tied to a pile under water and leading downward. In vain he had tried to heave up what was fast on the other end. Farther along, to another pile, was a similar rope, leading downward and unheavable. Without doubt, it was the missing salmon boat. If we restored it to its rightful owner there was fifty dollars in it for us. But I had queer ethical notions about honor amongst thieves, and declined to have anything to do with the affair.

But French Frank had quarreled with Whisky Bob, and Nelson was also an enemy. (Poor Whisky Bob!—without viciousness, good-natured, generous, born weak, raised poorly, with an irresistible chemical demand for alcohol, still prosecuting his vocation of bay pirate, his body was picked up, not long afterward, beside a dock where it had sunk full of gunshot wounds). Within an hour after I had rejected Captain Spink's proposal, I saw him sail down the estuary on board the *Reindeer* with Nelson. Also, French Frank went by on his schooner.

It was not long ere they sailed back up the estuary, curiously side by side. As they headed in for the sandpit, the submerged salmon boat could be seen, gunwales awash and held up from sinking by ropes fast to the schooner and the sloop. The tide was half out, and they sailed squarely in on the sand, grounding in a row with the salmon boat in the middle.

Immediately Hans, one of French Frank's sailors, was into a skiff and pulling rapidly for the north shore. The big demijohn in the stern-sheets told his errand. They could n't wait a moment to celebrate the fifty dollars they had so easily earned. It is the way of the devotees of John Barleycorn. When good fortune comes, they drink. When they have no fortune they drink to the hope of good fortune. If fortune be ill, they drink to forget it. If they meet a friend, they drink. If they quarrel with a friend and lose him, they drink. If their love-making be crowned with success, they are so happy they needs must drink. If they be jilted, they drink for the contrary reason. And if they have n't anything to do at all, why they take a drink, secure in the knowledge that when they have taken a sufficient number of drinks the maggots will start crawling in their brains and they will have their hands full with things to do. When they are sober they want to drink; and when they have drunk they want to drink more.

Of course, as fellow comrades, Scotty and I

were called in for the drinking. We helped to make a hole in that fifty dollars not yet received. The afternoon, from just an ordinary, common, summer, Sunday afternoon, became a gorgeous, purple afternoon. We all talked and sang and ranted and bragged, and ever French Frank and Nelson sent more drinks around. We lay in full sight of the Oakland water-front, and the noise of our revels attracted friends. Skiff after skiff crossed the estuary and hauled up on the sandpit, while Hans' work was cut out for him—ever to row back and forth for more supplies of booze.

Then Whisky Bob and Nicky the Greek arrived, sober, indignant, outraged in that their fellow pirates had raised their plant. French Frank, aided by John Barleycorn, orated hypocritically about virtue and honesty, and, despite his fifty years, got Whisky Bob out on the sand and proceeded to lick him. When Nicky the Greek jumped in with a short-handled shovel to Whisky Bob's assistance, short work was made of him by Hans. And of course, when the bleeding remnants of Bob and Nicky were sent packing in their skiff, the event must needs be celebrated in further carousal.

By this time, our visitors being numerous, we were a large crowd compounded of many nationalities and diverse temperaments, all aroused by John Barleycorn, all restraints cast off. Old quarrels revived, ancient hates flared up. Fight was in the air. And whenever a longshoreman remembered something against a scow-schooner sailor, or vice versa, or an oyster pirate remembered or was remembered, a fist shot out and another fight was on. And every fight was made up in more rounds of drinks, wherein the combatants, aided and abetted by the rest of us, embraced each other and pledged undying friendship.

And of all times, Soup Kennedy selected this time to come and retrieve an old shirt of his, left

aboard the *Reindeer* from the trip he sailed with
Clam. He had espoused Clam's side of the quarrel
with Nelson. Also, he had been drinking in the
St. Louis House, so that it was John Barleycorn
who led him to the sandpit in quest of his old
shirt. A few words started the fray. He locked
with Nelson in the cockpit of the *Reindeer*, and in
the mix-up barely escaped being brained by an
iron bar wielded by irate French Frank—irate because a two-handed man had attacked a one-
handed man. (If the *Reindeer* still floats, the dent
of the iron bar remains in the hard-wood rail of
her cockpit.)

But Nelson pulled his bandaged hand, bullet-
perforated, out of its sling, and, held by us, wept
and roared his Berserker belief that he could lick
Soup Kennedy one-handed. And we let them loose
on the sand. Once, when it looked as if Nelson
were getting the worst of it, French Frank and
John Barleycorn sprang unfairly into the fight.
Scotty protested and reached for French Frank,
who whirled upon him and fell on top of him in a
pummeling clinch after a sprawl of twenty feet
across the sand. In the course of separating these
two, half-a-dozen fights started amongst the rest
of us. These fights were finished, one way or the
other, or we separated them with drinks, while all
the time Nelson and Soup Kennedy fought on.
Occasionally we returned to them and gave advice, such as, when they lay exhausted in the
sand, unable to strike a blow, "Throw sand in his
eyes." And they threw sand in each other's eyes,
recuperated and fought on to successive exhaus-
tions.

And now, of all this that is squalid, and ridiculous, and bestial, try to think what it meant to me,
a youth not yet sixteen, burning with the spirit of
adventure, fancy-filled with tales of bucaneers and
sea-rovers, sacks of cities and conflicts of armed

men, and imagination-maddened by the stuff I had drunk. It was life raw and naked, wild and free—the only life of that sort which my birth in time and space permitted me to attain. And more than that. It carried a promise. It was the beginning. From the sandpit the way led out through the Golden Gate to the vastness of adventure of all the world, where battles would be fought, not for old shirts and over stolen salmon boats, but for high purposes and romantic ends.

And because I told Scotty what I thought of his letting an old man like French Frank get away with him, we, too, brawled and added to the festivity of the sandpit. And Scotty threw up his job as crew, and departed in the night with a pair of blankets belonging to me. During the night, while the oyster pirates lay stupefied in their bunks, the schooner and the *Reindeer* floated on the high water and swung about to their anchors. The salmon boat, still filled with rocks and water, rested on the bottom.

In the morning, early, I heard wild cries from the *Reindeer*, and tumbled out in the chill gray to see a spectacle that made the water-front laugh for days. The beautiful salmon boat lay on the hard sand, squashed flat as a pancake, while on it were perched French Frank's schooner and the *Reindeer*. Unfortunately two of the *Reindeer*'s planks had been crushed in by the stout oak stem of the salmon boat. The rising tide had flowed through the hole and just awakened Nelson by getting into his bunk with him. I lent a hand, and we pumped the *Reindeer* out and repaired the damage.

Then Nelson cooked breakfast, and while we ate we considered the situation. He was broke. So was I. The fifty dollars' reward would never be paid for that pitiful mess of splinters on the sand beneath us. He had a wounded hand and no crew. I had a burned mainsail and no crew. "What

d 'ye say you and me?" Nelson queried. "I 'll go
you," was my answer. And thus I became partners with "Young Scratch" Nelson, the wildest,
maddest of them all. We borrowed the money for
an outfit of grub from Johnny Heinhold, filled our
water-barrels, and sailed away that day for the
oyster-beds.

Chapter XII

NOR have I ever regretted those months of mad
deviltry I put in with Nelson. He *could* sail,
even if he did frighten every man that sailed with
him. To steer to miss destruction by an inch or an
instant was his joy. To do what everybody else
did not dare attempt to do was his pride. Never to
reef down was his mania, and in all the time I
spent with him, blow high or low, the *Reindeer*
was never reefed. Nor was she ever dry. We
strained her open and sailed her open and sailed
her open continually. And we abandoned the Oakland water-front and went wider afield for our
adventures.

And all this glorious passage in my life was
made possible for me by John Barleycorn. And
this is my complaint against John Barleycorn. Here
I was, thirsting for the wild life of adventure, and
the only way for me to win to it was through John
Barleycorn's mediation. It was the way of the men
who lived the life. Did I wish to live the life, I
must live it the way they did. It was by virtue of
drinking that I gained that partnership and comradeship with Nelson. Had I drunk only the beer
he paid for, or had I declined to drink at all, I
should never have been selected by him as a partner. He wanted a partner who would meet him
on the social side, as well as the work side, of life.

I abandoned myself to the life, and developed
the misconception that the secret of John Barley-

corn lay in going on mad drunks, rising through the successive stages that only an iron constitution could endure to final stupefaction and swinish unconsciousness. I did not like the taste, so I drank for the sole purpose of getting drunk, of getting hopelessly, helplessly drunk. And I, who had saved and scraped, traded like a Shylock and made junkmen weep; I, who had stood aghast when French Frank, at a single stroke, spent eighty cents for whisky for eight men; I turned myself loose with a more lavish disregard for money than any of them.

I remember going ashore one night with Nelson. In my pocket was one hundred and eighty dollars. It was my intention, first to buy me some clothes, after that some drinks. I needed the clothes. All I possessed were on me, and they were as follows: a pair of sea-boots that providentially leaked the water out as fast as it ran in, a pair of fifty-cent overalls, a forty-cent cotton shirt, and a sou'wester. I had no hat, so I had to wear the sou'wester, and it will be noted that I have listed neither underclothes nor socks. I didn't own any.

To reach the stores where clothes could be bought, we had to pass a dozen saloons. So I bought me the drinks first. I never got to the clothing stores. In the morning, broke, poisoned, but contented, I came back on board, and we set sail. I possessed only the clothes I had gone ashore in, and not a cent remained of the one hundred and eighty dollars. It might well be deemed impossible, by those who have never tried it, that in twelve hours a lad can spend all of one hundred and eighty dollars for drinks. I know otherwise.

And I had no regrets. I was proud. I had shown them I could spend with the rest of them. Amongst strong men I had proved myself strong. I had clinched again, as I had often clinched, my right to the title of "Prince." Also, my attitude may be

considered, in part, as a reaction from my childhood's meagerness and my childhood's excessive
toil.

Possibly my inchoate thought was: Better to
reign among booze-fighters, a prince, than to toil
twelve hours a day at a machine for ten cents an
hour. There are no purple passages in machine
toil. But if the spending of one hundred and eighty
dollars in twelve hours is n't a purple passage,
then I 'd like to know what is.

Oh, I skip much of the details of my trafficking
with John Barleycorn during this period, and shall
only mention events that will throw light on John
Barleycorn's ways. There were three things that
enabled me to pursue this heavy drinking: first, a
magnificent constitution far better than the average; second, the healthy, open-air life on the water; and third, the fact that I drank irregularly.
While out on the water, we never carried any
drink along.

The world was opening up to me. Already I
knew several hundred miles of the waterways of
it, and of the towns and cities and fishing hamlets
on the shores. Came the whisper to range farther.
I had not found it yet. There was more behind.
But even this much of the world was too wide for
Nelson. He wearied for his beloved Oakland water-
front, and when he elected to return to it we
separated in all friendliness.

I now made the old town of Benicia, on the
Carquinez Straits, my headquarters. In a cluster of
fishermen's arks, moored in the tules on the water-
front, dwelt a congenial crowd of drinkers and
vagabonds, and I joined them. I had longer spells
ashore, between fooling with salmon fishing and
making raids up and down bay and rivers as a
deputy fish patrolman, and I drank more and
learned more about drinking. I held my own with
any one, drink for drink; and often drank more

than my share to show the strength of my manhood. When, on a morning, my unconscious carcass was disentangled from the nets on the drying-frames, whither I had stupidly, blindly crawled the night before; and when the water-front talked it over with many a giggle and laugh and another drink, I was proud indeed. It was an exploit.

And when I never drew a sober breath, on one stretch, for three solid weeks, I was certain I had reached the top. Surely, in that direction, one could go no farther. It was time for me to move on. For always, drunk or sober, at the back of my consciousness something whispered that this carousing and bay-adventuring was not all of life. This whisper was my good fortune. I happened to be so made that I could hear it calling, always calling, out and away over the world. It was not canniness on my part. It was curiosity, desire to know, an unrest and a seeking for things wonderful that I seemed somehow to have glimpsed or guessed. What was this life for, I demanded, if this were all? No; there was something more, away and beyond. (And, in relation to my much later development as a drinker, this whisper, this promise of the things at the back of life, must be noted, for it was destined to play a dire part in my later wrestlings with John Barleycorn.)

But what gave immediacy to my decision to move on, was a trick John Barleycorn played me—a monstrous, incredible trick that showed abysses of intoxication hitherto undreamed. At one o'clock in the morning, after a prodigious drunk, I was tottering aboard a sloop at the end of the wharf, intending to go to sleep. The tides sweep through Carquinez Straits as in a mill-race, and the full ebb was on when I stumbled overboard. There was nobody on the wharf, nobody on the sloop. I was borne away by the current. I was not startled. I thought the misadventure delightful. I was a good swimmer, and in my inflamed condition the contact of the water with my skin soothed me like cool linen.

And then John Barleycorn played me his maniacal trick. Some maundering fancy of going out with the tide suddenly obsessed me. I had never been morbid. Thoughts of suicide had never entered my head. And now that they entered, I thought it fine, a splendid culmination, a perfect rounding off of my short but exciting career. I, who had never known girl's love, nor woman's love, nor the love of children; who had never played in the wide joy-fields of art, nor climbed the star-cool heights of philosophy, nor seen with my eyes more than a pin-point's surface of the gorgeous world; I decided that this was all, that I had seen all, lived all, been all, that was worth while, and that now was the time to cease. This was the trick of John Barleycorn, laying me by the heels of my imagination and in a drug-dream dragging me to death.

Oh, he was convincing. I had really experienced all of life, and it did n't amount to much. This swinish drunkenness in which I had lived for months (this was accompanied by the sense of degradation and the old feeling of conviction of sin) was the last and best, and I could see for myself what it was worth. There were all the broken-down old bums and loafers I had bought drinks for. That was what remained of life. Did I want to become like them? A thousand times no; and I wept tears of sweet sadness over my glorious youth going out with the tide. (And who has not seen the weeping-drunk, the melancholic drunk? They are to be found in all the barrooms, if they can find no other listener telling their sorrows to the barkeeper, who is paid to listen.)

The water was delicious. It was a man's way to die. John Barleycorn changed the tune he played in my drink-maddened brain. Away with tears and regret. It was a hero's death, and by the hero's own hand and will. So I struck up my death-chant and was singing it lustily, when the gurgle and splash of the current-riffles in my ears reminded me of my more immediate situation.

Below the town of Benicia, where the *Solano* wharf projects, the straits widen out into what bay-farers call the "Bight of Turner's Shipyard." I was in the shore-tide that swept under the *Solano* wharf and on into the bight. I knew of old the power of the suck which developed when the tide swung around the end of Dead Man's Island and drove straight for the wharf. I did n't want to go through those piles. It would n't be nice, and I might lose an hour in the bight on my way out with the tide.

I undressed in the water and struck out with a strong, single-overhand stroke, crossing the current at right angles. Nor did I cease until, by the wharf-lights, I knew I was safe to sweep by the end. Then I turned over and rested. The stroke had been a telling one, and I was a little time in recovering my breath.

I was elated, for I had succeeded in avoiding the suck. I started to raise my death-chant again—a purely extemporized farrago of a drug-crazed youth. "Don't sing . . . yet," whispered John Barleycorn. "The *Solano* runs all night. There are railroad men on the wharf. They will hear you, and come out in a boat and rescue you, and you don't want to be rescued." I certainly did n't. What? Be robbed of my hero's death? Never. And I lay on my back in the starlight, watching the familiar wharf-lights go by, red and green and white, and bidding sad, sentimental farewell to them, each and all.

When I was well clear, in mid-channel, I sang again. Sometimes I swam a few strokes, but in the main I contented myself with floating and dreaming long drunken dreams. Before daylight, the chill of the water and the passage of the hours had sobered me sufficiently to make me wonder what portion of the Straits I was in, and also to wonder if the turn of the tide would n't catch me and take me back ere I had drifted out into San Pablo Bay.

Next I discovered that I was very weary and very cold, and quite sober, and that I did n't in the least want to be drowned. I could make out the Selby Smelter on the Contra Costa shore and the Mare Island lighthouse. I started to swim for the Solano shore, but was too weak and chilled, and made so little headway, and at the cost of so painful effort that I gave it up and contented myself with floating, now and then giving a stroke to keep my balance in the tide-rips which were increasing their commotion on the surface of the water. And I knew fear. I was sober, now, and I did n't want to die. I discovered scores of reasons for living. And the more reasons I discovered, the more liable it seemed that I was going to drown anyway.

Daylight, after I had been four hours in the water, found me in a parlous condition in the tide-rips off Mare Island light, where the swift ebbs from Vallejo Straits and Carquinez Straits were fighting with each other, and where, at that particular moment, they were fighting the flood tide setting up against them from San Pablo Bay. A stiff breeze had sprung up, and the crisp little waves were persistently lapping into my mouth, and I was beginning to swallow salt water. With my swimmer's knowledge, I knew the end was near. And then the boat came—a Greek fisherman running in for Vallejo; and again I had been saved from John Barleycorn by my constitution and physical vigor.

And in passing, let me note that this maniacal trick John Barleycorn played me is nothing uncommon. An absolute statistic of the percentage of suicides due to John Barleycorn would be appalling. In my case, healthy, normal, young, full of the joy of life, the suggestion to kill myself was unusual; but it must be taken into account that it came on the heels of a long carouse, when my nerves and brain were fearfully poisoned, and that the dramatic, romantic side of my imagination, drink-maddened to lunacy, was delighted with the suggestion. And yet, the older, more morbid drinkers, more jaded with life and more disillusioned, who kill themselves, do so usually after a long debauch, when their nerves and brains are thoroughly poisoned-soaked.

Chapter XIII

So I LEFT BENICIA, where John Barleycorn had nearly got me, and ranged wider afield in pursuit of the whisper from the back of life to come and find. And wherever I ranged, the way lay along alcohol-drenched roads. Men still congregated in saloons. They were the poorman's clubs, and they were the only clubs to which I had access. I could get acquainted in saloons. I could go into a saloon and talk with any man. In the strange towns and cities I wandered through, the only place for me to go was the saloon. I was no longer a stranger in any town the moment I had entered a saloon.

And right here let me break in with experiences no later than last year. I harnessed four horses to a light trap, took Charmian along, and drove for three months and a half over the wildest mountain parts of California and Oregon. Each morning I did my regular day's work of writing fiction. That completed, I drove on through the middle of the day and the afternoon to the next stop. But the irregularity of occurrence of stopping places, coupled with widely varying road conditions, made it necessary to plan, the day before, each day's drive and my work. I must know when I was to start driving in order to start writing in time to finish my day's output. Thus, on occasion, when the drive was to be long, I would be up and at my writing by five in the morning. On easier driving days I might not start writing till nine o'clock.

But how to plan? As soon as I arrived in a town, and put the horses up, on the way from the stable to the hotel I dropped into the saloons. First thing, a drink—oh, I wanted the drink, but also it must not be forgotten that, because of wanting to know things, it was in this very way I had learned to want a drink. Well, the first thing, a drink. "Have something yourself," to the barkeeper. And then, as we drink, my opening query about roads and stopping-places on ahead.

"Let me see," the barkeeper will say, "there 's the road across Tarwater Divide. That used to be good. I was over it three years ago. But it was blocked this spring. . . . Say, I 'll tell you what. I 'll ask Jerry—" And the barkeeper turns and addresses some men sitting at a table or leaning against the bar farther along, and who may be Jerry, or Tom, or Bill. "Say, Jerry, how about the Tarwater road? You was down to Wilkins last week."

And while Bill or Jerry or Tom is beginning to unlimber his thinking and speaking apparatus, I suggest that he join us in the drink. Then discussions arise about the advisability of this road or that, what the best stopping places may be, what running time I may expect to make, where the best trout streams are, and so forth, in which other men join, and which are punctuated with more drinks.

Two or three more saloons, and I accumulate a warm jingle and come pretty close to knowing everybody in town, all about the town, and a fair deal about the surrounding country. I know the lawyers, editors, business men, local politicians, and the visiting ranchers, hunters, and miners, so that by evening, when Charmian and I stroll down the main street and back, she is astounded by the number of my acquaintances in that totally strange town.

And thus is demonstrated a service John Barleycorn renders, a service by which he increases his power over men. And over the world, wherever I have gone, during all the years, it has been the same. It may be a cabaret in the Latin Quarter, a café in some obscure Italian village, a boozing-ken in sailor-town, and it may be up at the club over Scotch and soda; but always it will be where John Barleycorn makes fellowship that I get immediately in touch, and meet, and know. And in the good days coming, when John Barleycorn will have been banished out of existence along with the other barbarians, some other institution than the saloon will have to obtain, some other congregating place of men where strange men and stranger men may get in touch, and meet, and know.

But to return to my narrative. When I turned my back on Benicia, my way led through saloons. I had developed no moral theories against drinking, and I disliked as much as ever the taste of the stuff. But I had grown respectfully suspicious of John Barleycorn. I could not forget that trick he had played on me—on *me*, who did not want to die. So I continued to drink, and to keep a sharp eye on John Barleycorn, resolved to resist all future suggestions of self-destruction.

In strange towns I made immediate acquaintances in the saloons. When I hoboed, and had n't the price of a bed, a saloon was the only place that would receive me and give me a chair by the fire. I could go into a saloon and wash up, brush my clothes, and comb my hair. And saloons were always so damnably convenient. They were everywhere in my western country.

I could n't go into the dwellings of strangers that way. Their doors were not open to me; no seats were there for me by their fires. Also, churches and preachers I had never known. And from what I did n't know I was not attracted toward them. Besides, there was no glamour about them, no haze of romance, no promise of adventure. They were the sort with whom things never happened. They lived and remained always in the one place, creatures of order and system, narrow, limited, restrained. They were without greatness, without imagination, without camaraderie. It was the good fellows, easy and genial, daring, and, on occasion, mad, that I wanted to know—the fellows, generous-hearted and handed, and not rabbit-hearted.

And here is another complaint I bring against John Barleycorn. It is these good fellows that he gets—the fellows with the fire and the go in them, who have bigness, and warmness, and the best of the human weaknesses. And John Barleycorn puts out the fire, and soddens the agility, and, when he does not more immediately kill them or make maniacs of them, he coarsens and grossens them, twists and malforms them out of the original goodness and fineness of their natures.

Oh!—and I speak out of later knowledge—heaven forefend me from the most of the average run of male humans who are not good fellows—the ones cold of heart and cold of head who don't smoke, drink, nor swear, nor do much of anything else that is brave, and resentful, and stinging, because in their feeble fibers there has never been the stir and prod of life to well over its boundaries and be devilish and daring. One does n't meet these in saloons, nor rallying to lost causes, nor flaming on the adventure-paths, nor loving as God's own mad lovers. They are too busy keeping their feet dry, conserving their heart-beats, and making unlovely life-successes of their spirit-mediocrity.

And so I draw the indictment home to John Barleycorn. It is just these, the good fellows, the worth while, the fellows with the weakness of too much strength, too much spirit, too much fire and flame of fine devilishness, that he solicits and ruins. Of course, he ruins weaklings; but with them, the worst we breed, I am not here concerned. My concern is that it is so much of the best we breed whom John Barleycorn destroys. And the reason why these best are destroyed is because John Barleycorn stands on every highway and byway, accessible, law-protected, saluted by the policeman on the beat, speaking to them, leading them by the hand to the places where the good fellows and daring ones foregather and drink deep. With John Barleycorn out of the way, these daring ones would still be born, and they would do things instead of perishing.

Always I encountered the camaraderie of drink. I might be walking down the track to the water-tank to lie in wait for a passing freight-train, when I would chance upon a bunch of "alki-stiffs." An alki-stiff is a tramp who drinks druggist's alcohol. Immediately, with greeting and salutation, I am taken into the fellowship. The alcohol, shrewdly blended with water, is handed to me, and soon I am caught up in the revelry, with maggots crawling in my brain and John Barleycorn whispering to me that life is big, and that we are all brave and fine—free spirits sprawling like careless gods upon the turf and telling the two-by-four, cut-and-dried, conventional world to go hang.

Chapter XIV

BACK IN OAKLAND from my wanderings, I returned to the water-front and renewed my comradeship with Nelson, who was now on shore all the time and living more madly than before. I, too, spent my time on shore with him, only occasionally going for cruises of several days on the bay to help out on short-handed scow-schooners.

The result was that I was no longer reinvigorated by periods of open-air abstinence and healthy toil. I drank every day, and whenever opportunity offered I drank to excess; for I still labored under the misconception that the secret of John Barleycorn lay in drinking to bestiality and unconsciousness. I became pretty thoroughly alcohol-soaked during this period. I practically lived in saloons; became a barroom loafer, and worse.

And right here was John Barleycorn getting me in a more insidious though no less deadly way than when he nearly sent me out with the tide. I had a few months still to run before I was seventeen; I scorned the thought of a steady job at anything; I felt myself a pretty tough individual in a group of pretty tough men; and I drank because these men drank and because I had to make good with them. I had never had a real boyhood, and in this, my precocious manhood, I was very hard and woefully wise. Though I had never known girl's love even, I had crawled through such depths that I was convinced absolutely that I knew the

last word about love and life. And it wasn't a
pretty knowledge. Without being pessimistic, I
was quite satisfied that life was a rather cheap and
ordinary affair.

You see, John Barleycorn was blunting me. The
old stings and prods of the spirit were no longer
sharp. Curiosity was leaving me. What did it matter what lay on the other side of the world? Men
and women, without doubt, very much like the
men and women I knew; marrying and giving in
marriage and all the petty human concerns; and
drinks, too. But the other side of the world was a
long way to go for a drink. I had but to step to the
corner and get all I wanted at Joe Vigy's. Johnny
Heinhold still ran the Last Chance. And there
were saloons on all the corners and between the
corners.

The whispers from the back of life were growing dim as my mind and body soddened. The old
unrest was drowsy. I might as well rot and die
here in Oakland as anywhere else. And I should
have so rotted and died and not in very long
order either, at the pace John Barleycorn was leading me, had the matter depended wholly on him.
I was learning what it was to have no appetite. I
was learning what it was to get up shaky in the
morning, with a stomach that quivered, with fingers touched with palsy, and to know the drinker's need for a stiff glass of whisky neat in order
to brace up. (Oh! John Barleycorn is a wizard
dopester. Brain and body, scorched and jangled
and poisoned, return to be tuned up by the very
poison that caused the damage.)

There is no end to John Barleycorn's tricks. He
had tried to inveigle me into killing myself. At
this period he was doing his best to kill me at a
fairly rapid pace. But not satisfied with that, he
tried another dodge. He very nearly got me, too,
and right there I learned a lesson about him—

became a wiser, a more skilful drinker. I learned there were limits to my gorgeous constitution, and that there were no limits to John Barleycorn. I learned that in a short hour or two he could master my strong head, my broad shoulders and deep chest, put me on my back, and with a devil's grip on my throat proceed to choke the life out of me.

Nelson and I were sitting in the Overland House. It was early in the evening, and the only reason we were there was because we were broke and it was election time. You see, in election time local politicians, aspirants for office, have a way of making the rounds of the saloons to get votes. One is sitting at a table, in a dry condition, wondering who is going to turn up and buy him a drink, or if his credit is good at some other saloon and if it's worth while to walk that far to find out, when suddenly the saloon doors swing wide and enters a bevy of well-dressed men, themselves usually wide and exhaling an atmosphere of prosperity and fellowship.

They have smiles and greetings for everybody— for you, without the price of a glass of beer in your pocket, for the timid hobo who lurks in the corner and who certainly has n't a vote but who may establish a lodging-house registration. And do you know, when these politicians swing wide the doors and come in, with their broad shoulders, their deep chests, and their generous stomachs which cannot help making them optimists and masters of life, why, you perk right up. It 's going to be a warm evening after all, and you know you 'll get a souse started at the very least. And—who knows?—the gods may be kind, other drinks may come, and the night culminate in glorious greatness. And the next thing you know, you are lined up at the bar, pouring drinks down your throat and learning the gentlemen's names and the offices which they hope to fill.

It was during this period, when the politicians went their saloon rounds, that I was getting bitter bits of education and having illusions punctured—I, who had pored and thrilled over "The Rail-Splitter," and "From Canal Boy to President." Yes, I was learning how noble politics and politicians are.

Well, on this night, broke, thirsty, but with the drinker's faith in the unexpected drink, Nelson and I sat in the Overland House waiting for something to turn up, especially politicians. And there entered Joe Goose—he of the unquenchable thirst, the wicked eyes, the crooked nose, the flowered vest.

"Come on, fellows—free booze—all you want of it. I did n't want you to miss it."

"Where?" we wanted to know.

"Come on. I 'll tell you as we go along. We have n't a minute to lose." And as we hurried up town, Joe Goose explained. "It 's the Hancock Fire Brigade. All you have to do is wear a red shirt and a helmet, and carry a torch. They 're going down on a special train to Haywards to parade."

(I think the place was Haywards. It may have been San Leandro or Niles. And, to save me, I can't remember whether the Hancock Fire Brigade was a Republican or a Democratic organization. But anyway, the politicians who ran it were short of torch-bearers, and anybody who would parade could get drunk if he wanted to.)

"The town 'll be wide open," Joe Goose went on. "Booze? It 'll run like water. The politicians have bought the stocks of the saloons. There 'll be no charge. All you got to do is walk right up and call for it. We 'll raise hell."

At the hall, on Eighth Street near Broadway, we got into the firemen's shirts and helmets, were equipped with torches, and, growling because we were n't given at least one drink before we started, were herded aboard the train. Oh, those politicians had handled our kind before. At Haywards there were no drinks either. Parade, first, and earn your booze, was the order of the night.

We paraded. Then the saloons were opened. Extra barkeepers had been engaged, and the drinkers jammed six deep before every drink-drenched and unwiped bar. There was no time to wipe the bar, nor wash glasses, nor do anything save fill glasses. The Oakland water-front can be real thirsty on occasion.

This method of jamming and struggling in front of the bar was too slow for us. The drink was ours. The politicians had bought it for us. We 'd paraded and earned it, had n't we? So we made a flank attack around the end of the bar, shoved the protesting barkeepers aside, and helped ourselves to bottles.

Outside, we knocked the necks of the bottles off against the concrete curbs and drank. Now Joe Goose and Nelson had learned discretion with straight whisky, drunk in quantity. I had n't: I still labored under the misconception that one was to drink all he could get—especially when it did n't cost anything. We shared our bottles with others, and drank a good portion ourselves, while I drank most of all. And I did n't like the stuff. I drank it as I had drunk beer at five, and wine at seven. I mastered my qualms and downed it like so much medicine. And when we wanted more bottles, we went into other saloons where the free drink was flowing, and helped ourselves.

I have n't the slightest idea of how much I drank—whether it was two quarts or five. I do know that I began the orgy with half-pint draughts and with no water afterward to wash the taste away and to dilute the whisky.

Now the politicians were too wise to leave the town filled with drunks from the water-front of Oakland. When train time came, there was a round-up of the saloons. Already I was feeling the impact of the whisky. Nelson and I were hustled out of a saloon, and found ourselves in the very last rank of a disorderly parade. I struggled along heroically, my correlations breaking down, my legs tottering under me, my head swimming, my heart pounding, my lungs panting for air.

My helplessness was coming on so rapidly that my reeling brain told me I would go down and out and never reach the train if I remained at the rear of the procession. I left the ranks and ran down a pathway beside the road under broad-spreading trees. Nelson pursued me, laughing. Certain things stand out, as in memories of nightmare. I remember those trees especially, and my desperate running along under them, and how, every time I fell, roars of laughter went up from the other drunks. They thought I was merely antic drunk. They did not dream that John Barleycorn had me by the throat in a death-clutch. But I knew it. And I remember the fleeting bitterness that was mine as I realized that I was in a struggle with death and that these others did not know. It was as if I were drowning before a crowd of spectators who thought I was cutting up tricks for their entertainment.

And running there under the trees, I fell and lost consciousness. What happened afterward, with one glimmering exception, I had to be told. Nelson, with his enormous strength, picked me up and dragged me on and aboard the train. When he had got me into a seat, I fought and panted so terribly for air that even with his obtuseness he knew I was in a bad way. And right there, at any moment, I know now, I might have died. I often think it is the nearest to death I have ever been. I have only Nelson's description of my behavior to go by.

I was scorching up, burning alive internally, in

an agony of fire and suffocation, and I wanted air.
I madly wanted air. My efforts to raise a window
were vain, for all the windows in the car were
screwed down. Nelson had seen drink-crazed men,
and thought I wanted to throw myself out. He
tried to restrain me, but I fought on. I seized some
man's torch and smashed the glass.

Now there were pro-Nelson and anti-Nelson
factions on the Oakland water-front, and men of
both factions, with more drink in them than was
good, filled the car. My smashing of the window
was the signal for the anti's. One of them reached
for me, and dropped me, and started the fight, of
all of which I have no knowledge save what was
told me afterward, and a sore jaw next day from
the blow that put me out. The man who struck
me went down across my body, Nelson followed
him, and they say there were few unbroken windows in the wreckage of the car that followed as
the free-for-all fight had its course.

This being knocked cold and motionless was
perhaps the best thing that could have happened
to me. My violent struggles had only accelerated
my already dangerously accelerated heart, and increased the need for oxygen in my suffocating
lungs.

After the fight was over and I came to, I did not
come to myself. I was no more myself than a
drowning man is who continues to struggle after
he has lost consciousness. I have no memory of
my actions, but I cried "Air! Air!" so insistently,
that it dawned on Nelson that I did not contem-
plate self-destruction. So he cleared the jagged
glass from the window ledge and let me stick my
head and shoulders out. He realized, partially,
the seriousness of my condition, and held me by
the waist to prevent me from crawling farther out.
And for the rest of the run in to Oakland I kept

my head and shoulders out, fighting like a maniac whenever he tried to draw me inside.

And here my one glimmering streak of true consciousness came. My sole recollection, from the time I fell under the trees until I awoke the following evening, is of my head out the window, facing the wind caused by the train, cinders striking and burning and blinding me, while I breathed with will. All my will was concentrated on breathing— on breathing the air in the hugest lung-full gulps I could, pumping the greatest amount of air into my lungs in the shortest possible time. It was that or death, and I was a swimmer and diver and I knew it; and in the most intolerable agony of prolonged suffocation, during those moments I was conscious, I faced the wind and the cinders and breathed for life.

All the rest is a blank. I came to the following evening, in a water-front lodging-house. I was alone. No doctor had been called in. And I might well have died there, for Nelson and the others, deeming me merely "sleeping off my drunk," had let me lie there in a comatose condition for seventeen hours. Many a man, as every doctor knows, has died of the sudden impact of a quart or more of whisky. Usually one reads of them so dying, strong drinkers, on account of a wager. But I did n't know . . . then. And so I learned; and by no virtue nor prowess, but simply through good fortune and constitution. Again my constitution had triumphed over John Barleycorn. I had escaped from another death-pit, dragged myself through another morass, and perilously acquired the discretion that would enable me to drink wisely for many another year to come.

Heavens! That was twenty years ago, and I am still very much and wisely alive; and I have seen much, done much, lived much, in that intervening score of years; and I shudder when I think how close a shave I ran, how near I was to missing that splendid fifth of a century that has been mine. And, oh, it was n't John Barleycorn's fault that he did n't get me that night of the Hancock Fire Brigade.

Chapter XV

IT WAS during the early winter of 1892 that I resolved to go to sea. My Hancock Fire Brigade experience was very little responsible for this. I still drank and frequented saloons—practically lived in saloons. Whisky was dangerous, in my opinion, but not wrong. Whisky was dangerous, like other dangerous things in the natural world. Men died of whisky; but then, too, fishermen were capsized and drowned, hoboes fell under trains and were cut to pieces. To cope with winds and waves, railroad trains, and barrooms, one must use judgment. To get drunk after the manner of men was all right, but one must do it with discretion. No more quarts of whisky for me.

What really decided me to go to sea was that I had caught my first vision of the death-road which John Barleycorn maintains for his devotees. It was not a clear vision, however, and there were two phases of it, somewhat jumbled at the time. It struck me, from watching those with whom I associated, that the life we were living was more destructive than that lived by the average man.

John Barleycorn, by inhibiting morality, incited to crime. Everywhere I saw men doing, drunk, what they would never dream of doing sober. And this was n't the worst of it. It was the penalty that must be paid. Crime was destructive. Saloonmates I drank with, who were good fellows and harmless, sober, did most violent and lunatic things when they were drunk. And then the police gathered them in and they vanished from our ken. Sometimes I visited them behind the bars and said good-by ere they journeyed across the bay to put on the felon's stripes. And time and again I heard the one explanation: *If I hadn't been drunk I wouldn't a-done it*. And sometimes, under the spell of John Barleycorn, the most frightful things were done—things that shocked even my case-hardened soul.

The other phase of the death-road was that of the habitual drunkards, who had a way of turning up their toes without apparent provocation. When they took sick, even with trifling afflictions that any ordinary man could pull through, they just pegged out. Sometimes they were found unattended and dead in their beds; on occasion their bodies were dragged out of the water; and sometimes it was just plain accident, as when Bill Kelly, unloading cargo while drunk, had a finger jerked off, which, under the circumstances, might just as easily have been his head.

So I considered my situation and knew that I was getting into a bad way of living. It made toward death too quickly to suit my youth and vitality. And there was only one way out of this hazardous manner of living and that was to get out. The sealing-fleet was wintering in San Francisco Bay, and in the saloons I met skippers, mates, hunters, boat-steerers, and boat-pullers. I met the seal-hunter, Pete Holt, and agreed to be his boat-puller and to sign on any schooner he signed on. And I had to have half-a-dozen drinks with Pete Holt there and then to seal our agreement.

And at once awoke all my old unrest that John Barleycorn had put to sleep. I found myself actually bored with the saloon-life of the Oakland water-front, and wondered what I had ever found fascinating in it. Also, with this death-road concept in my brain, I began to grow afraid that something would happen to me before sailing day, which was set for some time in January. I lived more circumspectly, drank less deeply, and went home more frequently. When drinking grew too wild, I got out. When Nelson was in his maniacal cups, I managed to get separated from him.

On the twelfth of January, 1893, I was seventeen, and the twentieth of January I signed before the shipping commissioner the articles of the *Sophie Sutherland*, a three topmast sealing schooner bound on a voyage to the coast of Japan. And of course we had to drink on it. Joe Vigy cashed my advance note, and Pete Holt treated, and I treated, and Joe Vigy treated, and other hunters treated. Well, it was the way of men, and who was I, just turned seventeen, that I should decline the way of life of these fine, chesty, man-grown men?

Chapter XVI

THERE WAS NOTHING to drink on the *Sophie Suth-erland*, and we had fifty-one days of glorious sailing, taking the southern passage in the north-east trades to Bonin Islands. This isolated group, belonging to Japan, had been selected as the ren-dezvous of the Canadian and American sealing-fleets. Here they filled their water-barrels and made repairs before starting on the hundred days' harry-ing of the seal-herd along the northern coasts of Japan to Behring Sea.

Those fifty-one days of fine sailing and intense sobriety had put me in splendid fettle. The alco-hol had been worked out of my system, and from the moment the voyage began I had not known the desire for a drink. I doubt if I ever thought once about a drink. Often, of course, the talk in the forecastle turned on drink, and the men told of their more exciting or humorous drunks, re-membering such passages more keenly, with greater delight, than all the other passages of their adventurous lives.

In the forecastle, the oldest man, fat and fifty, was Louis. He was a broken skipper. John Barley-corn had thrown him, and he was winding up his career where he had begun it, in the forecastle. His case made quite an impression on me. John Barleycorn did other things beside kill a man. He had n't killed Louis. He had done much worse. He had robbed him of power and place and comfort, crucified his pride, and condemned him to the hardship of the common sailor that would last as long as his healthy breath lasted, which promised to be for a long time.

We completed our run across the Pacific, lifted the volcanic peaks, jungle-clad, of the Bonin Islands, sailed in among the reefs to the land-locked harbor, and let our anchor rumble down where lay a score or more of sea-gipsies like ourself. The scents of strange vegetation blew off the tropic land. Aborigines, in queer outrigger canoes, and Japanese, in queerer sampans, paddled about the bay and came aboard. It was my first foreign land; I had won to the other side of the world, and I would see all I had read in the books come true. I was wild to get ashore.

Victor and Axel, a Swede and a Norwegian, and I planned to keep together. (And so well did we, that for the rest of the cruise we were known as the "Three Sports.") Victor pointed out a pathway that disappeared up a wild canyon, emerged on a steep, bare lava-slope, and thereafter appeared and disappeared, ever climbing, among the palms and flowers. We would go over that path, he said, and we agreed, and we would see beautiful scenery, and strange native villages, and find Heaven alone knew what adventure at the end. And Axel was keen to go fishing. The three of us agreed to that, too. We would get a sampan, and a couple of Japanese fishermen who knew the fishing grounds, and we would have great sport. As for me, I was keen for anything.

And then, our plans made, we rowed ashore over the banks of living coral and pulled our boat up the white beach of coral sand. We walked across the fringe of beach under the cocoanut palms and into the little town, and found several hundred riotous seamen from all the world, drinking prodigiously, singing prodigiously, dancing prodigiously—and all on the main street to the scandal of a helpless handful of Japanese police.

Victor and Axel said we'd have a drink before we started on our long walk. Could I decline to drink with these two chesty shipmates? Drinking together, glass in hand, put the seal on comradeship. It was the way of life. Our teetotaler owner-captain was laughed at, and sneered at, by all of us because of his teetotalism. I didn't in the least want a drink, but I did want to be a good fellow and a good comrade. Nor did Louis' case deter me, as I poured the biting, scorching stuff down my throat. John Barleycorn had thrown Louis to a nasty fall, but I was young. My blood ran full and red; I had a constitution of iron; and—well, youth ever grins scornfully at the wreckage of age.

Queer, fierce, alcoholic stuff it was that we drank. There was no telling where or how it had been manufactured—some native concoction, most likely. But it was hot as fire, pale as water, and quick as death with its kick. It had been filled into empty "square-face" bottles which had once contained Holland gin and which still bore the fitting legend: "Anchor Brand." It certainly anchored us. We never got out of the town. We never went fishing in the sampan. And though we were there ten days, we never trod that wild path along the lava-cliffs and among the flowers.

We met old acquaintances from other schooners, fellows we had met in the saloons of San Francisco before we sailed. And each meeting meant a drink; and there was much to talk about; and more drinks; and songs to be sung; and pranks and antics to be performed; until the maggots of imagination began to crawl, and it all seemed great and wonderful to me, these lusty, hard-bitten sea-rovers, of whom I made one, gathered in wassail on a coral strand. Old lines about knights at table in the great banquet-halls, and of those above the salt and below the salt, and of Vikings feasting fresh from sea and ripe for battle, came to me; and I knew that the old times were not dead and that we belonged to that self-same ancient breed.

By mid-afternoon Victor went mad with drink, and wanted to fight everybody and everything. I have since seen lunatics in the violent wards of asylums that seemed to behave in no wise different from Victor's way, save that perhaps he was more violent. Axel and I interfered as peace-makers, were roughed and jostled in the mix-ups, and finally, with infinite precaution and intoxicated cunning, succeeded in inveigling our chum down to the boat and in rowing him aboard our schooner.

But no sooner did Victor's feet touch the deck, than he began to clean up the ship. He had the strength of several men, and he ran amuck with it. I remember especially one man whom he got into the chain-boxes but failed to damage through inability to hit him. The man dodged and ducked, and Victor broke the knuckles of both his fists against the huge links of the anchor chain. By the time we dragged him out of that, his madness had shifted to the belief that he was a great swimmer, and the next moment he was overboard and demonstrating his ability by floundering like a sick porpoise and swallowing much salt water.

We rescued him, and by the time we got him below, undressed, and into his bunk, we were wrecks ourselves. But Axel and I wanted to see more of shore, and away we went, leaving Victor snoring. It was curious, the judgment passed on Victor by his shipmates, drinkers themselves. They shook their heads disapprovingly and muttered: "A man like that ought n't to drink." Now Victor was the smartest sailor and best-tempered shipmate in the forecastle. He was an all-around splendid type of seaman; his mates recognized his worth,

and respected him and liked him. Yet John Barleycorn metamorphosed him into a violent lunatic. And that was the very point these drinkers
made. They knew that drink—and drink with a
sailor is always excessive—made them mad, but
only mildly mad. Violent madness was objection-
able because it spoiled the fun of others and often
culminated in tragedy. From their standpoint, mild
madness was all right. But from the standpoint of
the whole human race, is not all madness objec-
tionable? And is there a greater maker of madness
of all sorts than John Barleycorn?

But to return. Ashore, snugly ensconced in a
Japanese house of entertainment, Axel and I compared bruises, and over a comfortable drink talked
of the afternoon's happenings. We liked the quiet-
ness of that drink and took another. A shipmate
dropped in, several shipmates dropped in, and
we had more quiet drinks. Finally, just as we had
engaged a Japanese orchestra, and as the first
strains of the *samisens* and *taikos* were rising,
through the paper-walls came a wild howl from
the street. We recognized it. Still howling, dis-
daining doorways, with bloodshot eyes and wildly
waving muscular arms, Victor burst upon us
through the fragile walls. The old amuck rage was
on him, and he wanted blood, anybody's blood.
The orchestra fled; so did we. We went through
doorways, and we went through paper-walls—
anything to get away.

And after the place was half wrecked, and we
had agreed to pay the damage, leaving Victor
partly subdued and showing symptoms of lapsing
into a comatose state, Axel and I wandered away
in quest of a quieter drinking-place. The main
street was a madness. Hundreds of sailors rol-
licked up and down. Because the chief of police
with his small force was helpless, the Governor of

the colony had issued orders to the captains to have all their men on board by sunset.

What! To be treated in such fashion! As the news spread among the schooners, they were emptied. Everybody came ashore. Men who had had no intention of coming ashore, climbed into the boats. The unfortunate governor's *ukase* had precipitated a general debauch for all hands. It was hours after sunset, and the men wanted to see anybody try to put them on board. They went around inviting the authorities to try to put them on board. In front of the governor's house they were gathered thickest, bawling sea-songs, circulating square-faces, and dancing uproarious Virginia reels and old-country dances. The police, including the reserves, stood in little forlorn groups, waiting for the command the governor was too wise to issue. And I thought this saturnalia was great. It was like the old days of the Spanish Main come back. It was license; it was adventure. And I was part of it, a chesty sea-rover along with all these other chesty sea-rovers among the paper houses of Japan.

The governor never issued the order to clear the streets, and Axel and I wandered on from drink to drink. After a time, in some of the antics, getting hazy myself, I lost him. I drifted along, making new acquaintances, downing more drinks, getting hazier and hazier. I remember, somewhere, sitting in a circle with Japanese fishermen, kanaka boat-steerers from our own vessels, and a young Danish sailor fresh from cowboying in the Argentine and with a penchant for native customs and ceremonials. And with due and proper and most intricate Japanese ceremonial, we of the circle drank *sake*, pale, mild, and lukewarm, from tiny porcelain bowls.

And, later, I remember the runaway apprentices—boys of eighteen and twenty, of middle class

English families, who had jumped their ships and apprenticeships in various ports of the world and drifted into the forecastles of the sailing schooners. They were healthy, smooth-skinned, clear-eyed, and they were young—youths like me, learning the way of their feet in the world of men. And they *were* men. No mild *sake* for them, but square-faces illicitly refilled with corrosive fire that flamed through their veins and burst into conflagrations in their heads. I remember a melting song they sang, the refrain of which was:

> 'T is but a little golden ring,
>   I give it to thee with pride,
> Wear it for your mother's sake
>   When you are on the tide.

They wept over it as they sang it, the graceless young scamps who had all broken their mothers' prides, and I sang with them, and wept with them, and luxuriated in the pathos and the tragedy of it, and struggled to make glimmering inebriated generalizations on life and romance. And one last picture I have, standing out very clear and bright in the midst of vagueness before and blackness afterward. We—the apprentices and I—are swaying and clinging to one another under the stars. We are singing a rollicking sea-song, all save one who sits on the ground and weeps; and we are marking the rhythm with waving square-faces. From up and down the street come far choruses of sea-voices similarly singing, and life is great, and beautiful, and romantic, and magnificently mad.

And next, after the blackness, I open my eyes in the early dawn to see a Japanese woman, solicitously anxious, bending over me. She is the port-pilot's wife, and I am lying in her doorway. I am chilled and shivering, sick with the after sickness of debauch. And I feel lightly clad. Those rascals of runaway apprentices! They have acquired the habit of running away. They have run away with my possessions. My watch is gone. My few dollars are gone. My coat is gone. So is my belt. And yes, my shoes.

And the foregoing is a sample of the ten days I spent in the Bonin Islands. Victor got over his lunacy, rejoined Axel and me, and after that we caroused somewhat more discreetly. And we never climbed that lava path among the flowers. The town and the square-faces were all we saw.

One who has been burned by fire must preach about the fire. I might have seen and healthily enjoyed a whole lot more of the Bonin Islands, if I had done what I ought to have done. But, as I see it, it is not a matter of what one ought to do, or ought not to do. It is what one *does* do. That is the everlasting, irrefragable fact. I did just what I did. I did what all those men did in the Bonin Islands. I did what millions of men over the world were doing at that particular point in time. I did it because the way led to it, because I was only a human boy, a creature of my environment, and neither an anemic nor a god. I was just human, and I was taking the path in the world that men took—men whom I admired, if you please; full-blooded men, lusty, breedy, chesty men, free spirits and anything but niggards in the way they foamed life away.

And the way was open. It was like an uncovered well in a yard where children play. It is small use to tell the brave little boys toddling their way along into knowledge of life that they must n't play near the uncovered well. They *will* play near it. Any parent knows that. And we know that a certain percentage of them, the livest and most daring, will fall into the well. The case is the same with John Barleycorn. All the no-saying and no-

preaching in the world will fail to keep men, and
youths growing into manhood, away from John
Barleycorn when John Barleycorn is everywhere
accessible, and where John Barleycorn is everywhere the connotation of manliness, and daring,
and great-spiritedness.

The only rational thing for the twentieth century folk to do is to cover up the well; to make the
twentieth century in truth the twentieth century,
and to relegate to the nineteenth century and all
the preceding centuries the things of those centuries, the witch-burnings, the intolerances, the
fetiches, and, not least among such barbarisms,
John Barleycorn.

Chapter XVII

NORTH WE RACED from the Bonin Islands to pick up the seal-herd, and north we hunted it for a hundred days into frosty, wintry weather and into and through vast fogs which hid the sun from us for a week at a time. It was wild and heavy work off the Siberian coast, without a drink or thought of drink. Then we sailed south to Yokohama, with a big catch of skins in our salt and a heavy pay-day coming.

I was eager to be ashore and see Japan, but the first day was devoted to ship's work, and not until evening did we sailors land. And here, by the very system of things, by the way life was organized and men transacted affairs, John Barleycorn reached out and tucked my arm in his. The captain had given money for us to the hunters, and the hunters were waiting in a certain Japanese public house for us to come and get it. We rode to the place in rickshaws. Our own crowd had taken possession of it. Drink was flowing. Everybody had money, and everybody was treating. After the hundred days of hard toil and absolute abstinence, in the pink of physical condition, bulging with health, overspilling with spirits that had been long pent by discipline and circumstance, of course we would have a drink or two. And after that we would see the town.

It was the old story. There were so many drinks to be drunk, and as the warm magic poured through our veins and mellowed our voices and affections we knew it was no time to make invidious distinctions—to drink with this shipmate and to decline to drink with that shipmate. We were all shipmates who had been through stress and storm together, who had pulled and hauled on the same sheets and tackles, relieved one another's wheels, lain out side by side on the same jibboom when she was plunging into it and looked to see who was missing when she cleared and lifted. So we drank with all, and all treated, and our voices rose, and we remembered a myriad kindly acts of comradeship, and forgot our fights and wordy squabbles, and knew one another for the best fellows in the world.

Well, the night was young when we arrived in that public house, and for all of that first night that public house was what I saw of Japan—a drinking place which was very like a drinking place at home or anywhere else over the world.

We lay in Yokohama harbor for two weeks, and about all we saw of Japan was its drinking places where sailors congregated. Occasionally, some one of us varied the monotony with a more exciting drunk. In such fashion I managed a real exploit by swimming off to the schooner one dark midnight and going soundly to sleep while the water-police searched the harbor for my body and brought my clothes out for identification.

Perhaps it was for things like that, I imagined, that men got drunk. In our little round of living what I had done was a noteworthy event. All the harbor talked about it. I enjoyed several days of fame among the Japanese boatmen and ashore in the pubs. It was a red letter event. It was an event to be remembered and narrated with pride. I remember it to-day, twenty years afterward, with a secret glow of pride. It was a purple passage, just as Victor's wrecking of the tea house in the Bonin

Islands and my being looted by the runaway apprentices were purple passages.

The point is that the charm of John Barleycorn was still a mystery to me. I was so organically a non-alcoholic that alcohol itself made no appeal; the chemical reactions it produced in me were not satisfying because I possessed no need for such chemical satisfaction. I drank because the men I was with drank, and because my nature was such that I could not permit myself to be less of a man than other men at their favorite pastime. And I still had a sweet tooth, and on privy occasions when there was no man to see, bought candy and blissfully devoured it.

We hove up anchor to a jolly chanty, and sailed out of Yokohama harbor for San Francisco. We took the northern passage, and with the stout west wind at our back made the run across the Pacific in thirty-seven days of brave sailing. We still had a big pay-day coming to us, and for thirty-seven days, without a drink to addle our mental processes, we incessantly planned the spending of our money.

The first statement of each man—ever an ancient one in homeward-bound forecastles—was: "No boarding-house sharks in mine." Next, in parentheses, was regret at having spent so much money in Yokohama. And after that, each man proceeded to paint his favorite phantom. Victor, for instance, said that immediately he landed in San Francisco he would pass right through the water-front and the Barbary Coast, and put an advertisement in the papers. His advertisement would be for board and room in some simple working-class family. "Then," said Victor, "I shall go to some dancing-school for a week or two, just to meet and get acquainted with the girls and fellows. Then I 'll get the run of the different dancing-crowds, and be invited to their homes, and to parties, and all that, and with the money I 've got I can last out till next January when I 'll go sealing again."

No; he was n't going to drink. He knew the way of it, particularly his way of it, wine in, wit out, and his money would be gone in no time. He had his choice, based on bitter experience, between three days' debauch among the sharks and harpies of the Barbary Coast and a whole winter of wholesome enjoyment and sociability, and there was n't any doubt of the way he was going to choose.

Said Axel Gunderson, who did n't care for dancing and social functions: "I 've got a good payday. Now I can go home. It is fifteen years since I 've seen my mother and all the family. When I pay off I shall send my money home to wait for me. Then I 'll pick a good ship bound for Europe, and arrive there with another pay-day. Put them together, and I 'll have more money than ever in my life before. I 'll be a prince at home. You have n't any idea how cheap everything is in Norway. I can make presents to everybody, and spend my money like what would seem to them a millionaire, and live a whole year there before I 'd have to go back to sea."

"The very thing I 'm going to do," declared Red John. "It 's three years since I 've received a line from home and ten years since I was there. Things are just as cheap in Sweden, Axel, as in Norway, and my folks are real country folks and farmers. I 'll send my pay-day home and ship on the same ship with you for around the Horn. We 'll pick a good one."

And as Axel Gunderson and Red John painted the pastoral delights and festive customs of their respective countries, each fell in love with the other's home place, and they solemnly pledged to make the journey together, and to spend, together, six months in the one's Swedish home and six months in the other's Norwegian home. And for the rest of the voyage they could hardly be pried apart, so infatuated did they become with discussing their plans.

Long John was not a home-body. But he was tired of the forecastle. No boarding-house sharks in his. He, too, would get a room in a quiet family, and he would go to a navigation school and study to be a captain. And so it went. Each man swore that for once he would be sensible and not squander his money. No boarding-house sharks, no sailor-town, no drink, was the slogan of our forecastle.

The men became stingy. Never was there such economy. They refused to buy anything more from the slop-chest. Old rags had to last, and they sewed patch upon patch, turning out what are called "homeward-bound patches" of the most amazing dimensions. They saved on matches, even, waiting till two or three were ready to light their pipes from the same match.

As we sailed up the San Francisco water-front, the moment the port doctors passed us the boarding-house runners were alongside in whitehall boats. They swarmed on board, each drumming for his own boarding-house, and each with a bottle of free whisky inside his shirt. But we waved them grandly and blasphemously away. We wanted none of their boarding-houses and none of their whisky. We were sober, thrifty sailormen, with better use for our money.

Came the paying off before the Shipping Commissioner. We emerged upon the sidewalk, each with a pocketful of money. About us, like buzzards, clustered the sharks and harpies. And we looked at each other. We had been seven months together, and our paths were separating. One last farewell rite of comradeship remained. (Oh, it was the way, the custom). "Come on, boys," said our sailing-master. There stood the inevitable adjacent saloon. There were a dozen saloons all around. And when we had followed the sailing-master into the one of his choice, the sharks were thick on the sidewalk outside. Some of them even ventured inside, but we would have nothing to do with them.

There we stood at the long bar—the sailing-master, the mates, the six hunters, the six boat-steerers, and the five boat-pullers. There were only five of the last, for one of our number had been dropped overboard, with a sack of coal at his feet, between two snow squalls in a driving gale off Cape Jerimo. There were nineteen of us, and it was to be our last drink together. With seven months of men's work in the world, blow high, blow low, behind us, we were looking on each other for the last time. We knew it, for sailors' ways go wide. And the nineteen of us drank the sailing-master's treat. Then the mate looked at us with eloquent eyes and called for another round. We liked the mate just as well as the sailing-master, and we liked them both. Could we drink with one, and not the other?

And Pete Holt, my own hunter (lost next year in the *Mary Thomas* with all hands), called a round. The time passed, the drinks continued to come on the bar, our voices rose, and the maggots began to crawl. There were six hunters, and each insisted, in the sacred name of comradeship, that all hands drink with him just once. There were six boat-steerers and five boat-pullers and the same logic held with them. There was money in all our pockets, and our money was as good as any man's, and our hearts were as free and generous.

Nineteen rounds of drinks. What more would John Barleycorn ask in order to have his will with men? They were ripe to forget their dearly cherished plans. They rolled out of the saloon and into the arms of the sharks and harpies. They did n't last long. From two days to a week saw the end of their money and saw them being carted by the boarding-house master on board outward-bound ships. Victor was a fine body of a man, and through a lucky friendship managed to get into the life-saving service. He never saw the dancing-school nor placed his advertisement for a room in a working-class family. Nor did Long John win to navigation-school. By the end of the week he was a transient lumper on a river steamboat. Red John and Axel did not send their paydays home to the old country. Instead, and along with the rest, they were scattered on board sailing ships bound for the four quarters of the globe, where they had been placed by the boarding-house masters and where they were working out advance money which they had neither seen nor spent.

What saved me was that I had a home and people to go to. I crossed the bay to Oakland, and, among other things, took a look at the death-road. Nelson was gone—shot to death while drunk and resisting the officers. His partner in that affair was lying in prison. Whisky Bob was gone. Old Cole, Old Smoudge and Bob Smith were gone. Another Smith, he of the belted guns and the *Annie*, was drowned. French Frank, they said, was lurking up river, afraid to come down because of something he had done. Others were wearing stripes in San Quentin or Folsom. Big Alec, the King of the Greeks, whom I had known well in the old Benicia days, and with whom I had drunk whole nights through, had killed two men and fled to foreign parts. Fitzsimmons, with whom I had sailed on the Fish Patrol, had been stabbed in the lung through the back and had died a lingering death from tuberculosis. And so it went, a very lively and well-patronized road, and, from what I knew of all of them, John Barleycorn was responsible, with the sole exception of Smith of the *Annie*.

Chapter XVIII

MY INFATUATION for the Oakland water-front was quite dead. I did n't like the looks of it nor the life. I did n't care for the drinking, nor the vagrancy of it, and I wandered back to the Oakland Free Library and read the books with greater understanding. Then, too, my mother said I had sown my wild oats and it was time I settled down to a regular job. Also, the family needed the money. So I got a job at the jute mills—a ten-hour day at ten cents an hour. Despite my increase in strength and general efficiency, I was receiving no more than when I worked in the cannery several years before. But, then, there was a promise of a raise to a dollar and a quarter a day after a few months.

And here, so far as John Barleycorn is concerned, began a period of innocence. I did not know what it was to take a drink from month end to month end. Not yet eighteen years old, healthy and with labor-hardened but unhurt muscles, like any young animal I needed diversion, excitement, something beyond the books and the mechanical toil.

I strayed into Young Men's Christian Associations. The life there was healthful and athletic, but too juvenile. For me it was too late. I was not boy, nor youth, despite my paucity of years. I had bucked big with men. I knew mysterious and violent things. I was from the other side of life so far as concerned the young men I encountered in

124

the Y.M.C.A. I spoke another language, possessed a sadder and more terrible wisdom. (When I come to think it over, I realize, now, that I have never had a boyhood.) At any rate, the Y.M.C.A. young men were too juvenile for me, too unsophisticated. This I would not have minded, could they have met me and helped me mentally. But I had got more out of the books than they. Their meager physical experiences, plus their meager intellectual experiences, made a negative sum so vast that it overbalanced their wholesome morality and healthful sports.

In short, I could n't play with the pupils of a lower grade. All the clean splendid young life that was theirs was denied me—thanks to my earlier tutelage under John Barleycorn. I knew too much too young. And yet, in the good time coming, when alcohol is eliminated from the needs and the institutions of men, it will be the Y.M.C.A., and similar unthinkably better and wiser and more virile congregating places, that will receive the men who now go to saloons to find themselves and one another. In the meantime, we live to-day, here and now, and we discuss to-day, here and now.

I was working ten hours a day in the jute mills. It was humdrum machine-toil. I wanted life. I wanted to realize myself in other ways than at a machine for ten cents an hour. And yet I had had my fill of saloons. I wanted something new. I was growing up. I was developing unguessed and troubling potencies and proclivities. And at this very stage, fortunately, I met Louis Shattuck and we became chums.

Louis Shattuck, without one vicious trait, was a real innocently devilishly young fellow who was quite convinced that he was a sophisticated town-boy. And I was n't a town-boy at all. Louis was handsome, and graceful, and filled with love for the girls. With him it was an exciting and all-absorbing pursuit. I did n't know anything about girls. I had been too busy being a man. This was an entirely new phase of existence which had escaped me. And when I saw Louis say good-by to me, raise his hat to a girl of his acquaintance, and walk on by her side down the sidewalk, I was made excited and envious. I, too, wanted to play this game.

"Well—there 's only one thing to do," said Louis, "and that is, you must get a girl."

Which is more difficult than it sounds. Let me show you, at the expense of a slight going aside. Louis did not know girls in their home life. He had the entrée to no girl's home. And of course, I, a stranger in this new world, was similarly circumstanced. But further, Louis and I were unable to go to dancing-schools, or to public dances, which were very good places for getting acquainted. We did n't have the money. He was a blacksmith's apprentice, and was earning but slightly more than I. We both lived at home and paid our way. When we had done this, and bought our cigarettes, and the inevitable clothes and shoes, there remained to each of us, for personal spending, a sum that varied between seventy cents and a dollar for the week. We whacked this up, shared it, and sometimes loaned all of what was left of it when one of us needed it for some more gorgeous girl-adventure, such as car-fare out to Blair's Park and back—twenty cents, bang, just like that; and ice-cream for two—thirty cents; or tamales, which came cheaper and which for two cost only twenty cents.

I did not mind this money meagerness. The disdain for money I had learned from the oyster pirates had never left me. I did n't care over-weeningly for it for personal gratification; and in my philosophy I completed the circle, finding my-

self as equable with the lack of a ten-cent piece as
I was with the squandering of scores of dollars in
calling all men and hangers-on up to the bar to
drink with me.

But how to get a girl? There was no girl's home
to which Louis could take me and where I might
be introduced to girls. I knew none. And Louis'
several girls he wanted for himself; and anyway,
in the very human nature of boys' and girls' ways,
he could n't turn any of them over to me. He did
persuade them to bring girlfriends for me; but I
found them weak sisters, pale and ineffectual alongside the choice specimens he had.

"You 'll have to do like I did," he said finally. "I
got these by getting them. You 'll have to get one
the same way."

And he initiated me. It must be remembered
that Louis and I were hard situated. We really had
to struggle to pay our board and maintain a decent appearance. We met each other in the evening, after the day's work, on the street corner, or
in a little candy store on a side street, our sole
frequenting place. Here we bought our cigarettes,
and, occasionally, a nickel's worth of "red-hots."
(Oh, yes; Louis and I unblushingly ate candy—all
we could get. Neither of us drank. Neither of us
ever went into a saloon.)

But the girl. In quite primitive fashion, as Louis
advised me, I was to select her and make myself
acquainted with her. We strolled the streets in the
early evenings. The girls, like us, strolled in pairs.
And strolling girls *will* look at strolling boys
who look. (And to this day, in any town, city, or
village, in which I, in my middle age find myself,
I look on with the eye trained of old experience,
and watch the sweet game played by the strolling
boys and girls who just *must* stroll when the spring
and summer evenings call.)

The trouble was that in this Arcadian phase of

my history, I, who had come through, case-hardened, from the other side of life, was timid and bashful. Again and again Louis nerved me up. But I did n't know girls. They were strange and wonderful to me after my precocious man's life. I failed of the bold front and the necessary forwardness when the crucial moment came.

Then Louis would show me how—a certain, eloquent glance of eye, a smile, a daring, lifted hat, a spoken word, hesitancies, giggles, coy nervousness, and, behold, Louis acquainted and nodding me up to be introduced. But, when we paired off to stroll along boy and girl together, I noted that Louis had invariably picked the good-looker and left to me the little lame sister.

I improved, of course, after experiences too numerous to enter upon, so that there were divers girls to whom I could lift my hat and who would walk beside me in the early evenings. But girl's love did not immediately come to me. I was excited, interested, and I pursued the quest. And the thought of drink never entered my mind. Some of Louis' and my adventures have since given me serious pause when casting sociological generalizations. But it was all good and innocently youthful, and I learned one generalization, biological rather than sociological, namely, that the "Colonel's lady and Judy O'Grady are sisters under their skins."

And before long I learned girl's love, all the dear fond deliciousness of it, all the glory and the wonder. I shall call her Haydee. She was between fifteen and sixteen. Her little skirt reached her shoe-tops. We sat side by side in a Salvation Army meeting. She was not a convert, nor was her aunt, who sat on the other side of her and who, visiting from the country, where at that time the Salvation Army was not, had dropped in to the meeting for half an hour out of curiosity. And

Louis sat beside me and observed—I do believe he did no more than observe, because Haydee was not his style of girl.

We did not speak, but in that great half-hour we glanced shyly at each other, and shyly avoided or as shyly returned and met each other's glances more than several times. She had a slender oval face. Her brown eyes were beautiful. Her nose was a dream, as was her sweet-lipped, petulant-hinting mouth. She wore a tam o'shanter, and I thought her brown hair the prettiest shade of brown I had ever seen. And from that single experience of half an hour I have ever since been convinced of the reality of love at first sight.

All too soon the aunt and Haydee departed. (This is permissible at any stage of a Salvation Army meeting.) I was no longer interested in the meeting, and after an appropriate interval of a couple of minutes or less, started to leave with Louis. As we passed out, at the back of the hall a woman recognized me with her eyes, arose, and followed me. I shall not describe her. She was of my own kind and friendship of the old time on the water-front. When Nelson was shot, he had died in her arms, and she knew me as his one comrade. And she must tell me how Nelson had died, and I did want to know; so I went with her across the width of life from dawning boy's love for a brown-haired girl in a tam o'shanter back to the old sad savagery I had known.

And when I had heard the tale, I hurried away to find Louis, fearing that I had lost my first love with the first glimpse of her. But Louis was dependable. Her name was—Haydee. He knew where she lived. Each day she passed the blacksmith-shop where he worked, going to or from the Lafayette school. Further, he had seen her on occasion with Ruth, another schoolgirl; and, still further, Nita, who sold us red-hots at the candy store, was a friend of Ruth. The thing to do was to go around to the candy store and see if we could get Nita to give a note to Ruth to give to Haydee. If that could be arranged, all I had to do was write the note.

And it so happened. And in stolen half-hours of meeting I came to know all the sweet madness of boy's love and girl's love. So far as it goes it is not the biggest love in the world, but I do dare to assert that it is the sweetest. Oh, as I look back on it! Never did girl have more innocent boy-lover than I who had been so wicked-wise and violent beyond my years. I did n't know the first thing about girls. I, who had been hailed Prince of the Oyster Pirates, who could go anywhere in the world as a man amongst men; who could sail boats, lay aloft in black and storm, or go into the toughest hangouts in sailor town and play my part in any rough-house that started or call all hands to the bar—I did n't know the first thing I might say or do with this slender little chit of a girl-woman whose scant skirt just reached her shoe-tops and who was as abysmally ignorant of life, as I was, or thought I was, profoundly wise.

I remember we sat on a bench in the starlight. There was fully a foot of space between us. We slightly faced each other, our near elbows on the back of the bench; and once or twice our elbows just touched. And all the time, deliriously happy, talking in the gentlest and most delicate terms that might not offend her sensitive ears, I was cudgeling my brains in an effort to divine what I was expected to do. What did girls expect of boys, sitting on a bench and tentatively striving to find out what love was? What did she expect me to do? Was I expected to kiss her? Did she expect me to try? And if she did expect me, and I did n't, what would she think of me?

Ah, she was wiser than I—I know it now—the

little innocent girl-woman in her shoe-top skirt. She had known boys all her life. She encouraged me in the ways a girl may. Her gloves were off and in one hand, and I remember, lightly and daringly, in mock reproof for something I had said, how she tapped my lips with a tiny flirt of those gloves. I was like to swoon with delight. It was the most wonderful thing that had ever happened to me. And I remember yet the faint scent that clung to those gloves and that I breathed in the moment they touched my lips.

Then came the agony of apprehension and doubt. Should I imprison in my hand that little hand with the dangling, scented gloves which had just tapped my lips? Should I dare to kiss her there and then, or slip my arm around her waist? Or dared I even sit closer?

Well, I did n't dare. I did nothing. I merely continued to sit there and love with all my soul. And when we parted that evening I had not kissed her. I do remember the first time I kissed her, on another evening, at parting—a mighty moment, when I took all my heart of courage and dared. We never succeeded in managing more than a dozen stolen meetings, and we kissed perhaps a dozen times—as boys and girls kiss, briefly and innocently, and wonderingly. We never went anywhere—not even to a matinée. We once shared together five cents' worth of red-hots. But I have always fondly believed that she loved me. I know I loved her; and I dreamed day dreams of her for a year and more, and the memory of her is very dear.

Chapter XIX

WHEN I WAS with folk who did not drink, I never thought of drinking. Louis did not drink. Neither he nor I could afford it; but, more significant than that, we had no desire to drink. We were healthy, normal, non-alcoholic. Had we been alcoholic, we would have drunk whether or not we could have afforded it.

Each night, after the day's work, washed up, clothes changed and supper eaten, we met on the street corner or in the little candy store. But the warm, fall weather passed, and on bitter nights of frost or damp nights of drizzle the street corner was not a comfortable meeting place. And the candy store was unheated. Nita, or whoever waited on the counter, between waitings lurked in a back living-room that was heated. We were not admitted to this room, and in the store it was as cold as out-of-doors.

Louis and I debated the situation. There was only one solution: the saloon, the congregating place of men, the place where men hobnobbed with John Barleycorn. Well do I remember the damp and draughty evening, shivering without overcoats because we could not afford them, that Louis and I started out to select our saloon. Saloons are always warm and comfortable. Now Louis and I did not go into this saloon because we wanted a drink. Yet we knew that saloons were not charitable institutions. A man could not make a lounging place of a saloon without occasionally buying something over the bar.

Our dimes and nickels were few. We could ill spare any of them when they were so potent in buying carfare for oneself and a girl. (We never paid carfare when by ourselves, being content to walk.) So, in this saloon, we desired to make the most of our expenditure. We called for a deck of cards and sat down at a table and played euchre for an hour, in which time Louis treated once, and I treated once, to beer—the cheapest drink, ten cents for two. Prodigal! How we grudged it!

We studied the men who came into the place. They seemed all middle-aged and elderly work-men, most of them Germans, who flocked by themselves in old-acquaintance groups, and with whom we could have only the slightest contacts. We voted against that saloon, and went out cast-down with the knowledge that we had lost an evening and wasted twenty cents for beer that we did n't want.

We made several more tries on succeeding nights, and at last found our way into the Na-tional, a saloon on Tenth and Franklin. Here was a more congenial crowd. Here Louis met a fellow or two he knew, and here I met fellows I had gone to school with when a little lad in knee pants. We talked of old days, and of what had become of this fellow, and what that fellow was doing now, and of course we talked it over drinks. They treated, and we drank. Then, according to the code of drinking, we had to treat. It hurt, for it meant forty to fifty cents a clatter.

We felt quite enlivened when the short evening was over; but at the same time we were bankrupt. Our week's spending-money was gone. We de-cided that that was the saloon for us, and we agreed to be more circumspect thereafter in our drink-buying. Also, we had to economize for the rest of the week. We did n't even have carfare. We were compelled to break an engagement with two girls from West Oakland with whom we were attempting to be in love. They were to meet us up town the next evening, and we had n't the carfare necessary to take them home. Like many others financially embarrassed, we had to disappear for a time from the gay whirl—at least until Saturday night pay-day. So Louis and I rendezvoused in a livery stable, and with coats buttoned and chattering teeth played euchre and casino until the time of our exile was over.

Then we returned to the National Saloon and spent no more than we could decently avoid spending for the comfort and warmth. Sometimes we had mishaps, as when one got stuck twice in succession in a five-handed game of Sancho Pedro for the drinks. Such a disaster meant anywhere between twenty-five to eighty cents, just according to how many of the players ordered ten-cent drinks. But we could temporarily escape the evil effects of such disaster by virtue of an account we ran behind the bar. Of course, this only set back the day of reckoning and seduced us into spending more than we would have spent on a cash basis. (When I left Oakland suddenly for the adventure-path the following spring, I well remember I owed that saloon keeper one dollar and seventy cents. Long after, when I returned, he was gone. I still owe him that dollar and seventy cents, and if he should chance to read these lines I want him to know that I'll pay on demand.)

The foregoing incident of the National Saloon I have given in order again to show the lure, or draw, or compulsion, toward John Barleycorn in society as at present organized with saloons on all the corners. Louis and I were two healthy youths. We did n't want to drink. We could n't afford to drink. And yet we were driven by the circum-

stances of cold and rainy weather to seek refuge
in a saloon, where we had to spend part of our
pitiful dole for drink. It will be urged by some
critics that we might have gone to the Y.M.C.A.,
to night school, and to the social circles and homes
of young people. The only reply is that we did
n't. That is the irrefragable fact. We did n't. And
to-day, at this moment, there are hundreds of
thousands of boys like Louis and me doing just
what Louis and I did, with John Barleycorn, warm
and comfortable, beckoning and welcoming, tuck-
ing their arms in his and beginning to teach them
his mellow ways.

Chapter XX

THE JUTE MILLS failed of its agreement to increase my pay to a dollar and a quarter a day, and I, a free-born American boy whose direct ancestors had fought in all the wars from the old pre-Revolutionary Indian wars down, exercised my sovereign right of free contract by quitting the job.

I was still resolved to settle down, and I looked about me. One thing was clear. Unskilled labor did n't pay. I must learn a trade, and I decided on electricity. The need for electricians was constantly growing. But how to become an electrician? I had n't the money to go to a technical school or university; besides, I did n't think much of schools. I was a practical man in a practical world. Also, I still believed in the old myths which were the heritage of the American boy when I was a boy.

A canal boy could become a president. Any boy, who took employment with any firm, could, by thrift, energy, and sobriety, learn the business and rise from position to position until he was taken in as a junior partner. After that the senior partnership was only a matter of time. Very often—so ran the myth—the boy, by reason of his steadiness and application, married his employer's daughter. By this time I had been encouraged to such faith in myself in the matter of girls that I was quite certain I would marry my employer's daughter. There was n't a doubt of it. All the little boys in the myths did it as soon as they were old enough.

So I bade farewell forever to the adventure-path, and went out to the power-plant of one of our Oakland street-railways. I saw the superintendent himself, in a private office so fine that it almost stunned me. But I talked straight up. I told him I wanted to become a practical electrician, that I was unafraid of work, that I was used to hard work, and that all he had to do was look at me to see I was fit and strong. I told him that I wanted to begin right at the bottom and work up, that I wanted to devote my life to this one occupation and this one employment.

The superintendent beamed as he listened. He told me that I was the right stuff for success, and that he believed in encouraging American youth that wanted to rise. Why, employers were always on the lookout for young fellows like me, and alas, they found them all too rarely. My ambition was fine and worthy, and he would see to it that I got my chance. (And as I listened with swelling heart, I wondered if it was his daughter I was to marry.)

"Before you can go out on the road and learn the more complicated and higher details of the profession," he said, "you will, of course, have to work in the car house with the men who install and repair the motors. (By this time I was sure that it was his daughter, and I was wondering how much stock he might own in the company.)

"But," he said, "as you yourself so plainly see, you could n't expect to begin as a helper to the car house electricians. That will come when you have worked up to it. You will really begin at the bottom. In the car house your first employment will be sweeping up, washing the windows, keeping things clean. And after you have shown yourself satisfactory at that, then you may become a helper to the car house electricians."

I did n't see how sweeping and scrubbing a

building was any preparation for the trade of electrician; but I did know that in the books all the boys started with the most menial tasks and by making good ultimately won to the ownership of the whole concern.

"When shall I come to work?" I asked, eager to launch on this dazzling career.

"But," said the superintendent, "as you and I have already agreed, you must begin at the bottom. Not immediately can you in any capacity enter the car house. Before that you must pass through the engine room as an oiler."

My heart went down slightly and for the moment, as I saw the road lengthen between his daughter and me; then it rose again. I would be a better electrician with knowledge of steam engines. As an oiler in the great engine room I was confident that few things concerning steam would escape me. Heavens! My career shone more dazzling than ever.

"When shall I come to work?" I asked gratefully.

"But," said the superintendent, "you could not expect to enter immediately into the engine room. There must be preparation for that. And through the fire room, of course. Come, you see the matter clearly, I know. And you will see that even the mere handling of coal is a scientific matter and not to be sneezed at. Do you know that we weigh every pound of coal we burn? Thus, we learn the value of the coal we buy; we know to a tee the last penny of cost of every item of production, and we learn which firemen are the most watchful, which firemen, out of stupidity or carelessness, get the least out of the coal they fire." The superintendent beamed again. "You see how very important the little matter of coal is, and by as much as you learn of this little matter you will become that much better a workman—more valuable to us,

more valuable to yourself. Now, are you prepared
to begin?"

"Any time," I said valiantly. "The sooner the
better."

"Very well," he answered. "You will come to-
morrow morning at seven o'clock."

I was taken out and shown my duties. Also, I
was told the terms of my employment—a ten-
hour day, every day in the month including Sundays and holidays, with one day off each month,
with a salary of thirty dollars a month. It was n't
exciting. Years before, at the cannery, I had earned
a dollar a day for a ten-hour day. I consoled myself with the thought that the reason my earning
capacity had not increased with my years and
strength was because I had remained an unskilled
laborer. But it was different now. I was beginning
to work for skill, for a trade, for career and fortune and the superintendent's daughter.

And I was beginning in the right way—right at
the beginning. That was the thing. I was passing
coal to the firemen, who shoveled it into the fur-
naces where its energy was transformed into steam,
which, in the engine room, was transformed into
the electricity with which the electricians worked.
This passing of coal was surely the very beginning
. . . unless the superintendent should take it into
his head to send me to work in the mines from
which the coal came in order to get a complete
understanding of the genesis of electricity for street
railways.

Work! I, who had worked with men, found that
I did n't know the first thing about real work. A
ten-hour day! I had to pass coal for the day and
night shifts, and despite working through the noon-
hour, I never finished my task before eight at
night. I was working a twelve- to thirteen-hour
day, and I was n't being paid overtime as in the
cannery.

I might as well give the secret away right here. I was doing the work of two men. Before me, one mature able-bodied laborer had done the day shift and another equally mature able-bodied laborer had done the night shift. They had received forty dollars a month each. The superintendent, bent on an economical administration, had persuaded me to do the work of both men for thirty dollars a month. I thought he was making an electrician of me. In truth and fact, he was saving fifty dollars a month operating expenses to the company.

But I did n't know I was displacing two men. Nobody told me. On the contrary, the superintendent warned everybody not to tell me. How valiantly I went at it that first day. I worked at top speed, filling the iron wheelbarrow with coal, running it on the scales and weighing the load, then trundling it into the fire room and dumping it on the plates before the fires.

Work! I did more than the two men whom I had displaced. They had merely wheeled in the coal and dumped it on the plates. But while I did this for the day coal, the night coal I had to pile against the wall of the fire room. Now the fire room was small. It had been planned for a night coat-passer. So I had to pile the night coal higher and higher, buttressing up ʾ heap with stout planks. Toward the top of the neap I had to handle the coal a second time, tossing it up with a shovel.

I dripped with sweat, but I never ceased from my stride, though I could feel exhaustion coming on. By ten o'clock in the morning, so much of my body's energy had I consumed, I felt hungry and snatched a thick double-slice of bread and butter from my dinner pail. This I devoured, standing, grimed with coal dust, my knees trembling under me. By eleven o'clock, in this fashion, I had consumed my whole lunch. But what of it? I realized that it would enable me to continue working through the noon hour. And I worked all afternoon. Darkness came on, and I worked under the electric lights. The day fireman went off and the night fireman came on. I plugged away.

At half-past eight, famished, tottering, I washed up, changed my clothes, and dragged my weary body to the car. It was three miles to where I lived, and I had received a pass with the stipulation that I could sit down as long as there were no paying passengers in need of a seat. As I sank into a corner outside seat I prayed that no passenger might require my seat. But the car filled up, and, half way in, a woman came on board, and there was no seat for her. I started to get up, and to my astonishment found that I could not. With the chill wind blowing on me, my spent body had stiffened into the seat. It took me the rest of the run to unkink my complaining joints and muscles and get into a standing position on the lower step. And when the car stopped at my corner I nearly fell to the ground when I stepped off.

I hobbled two blocks to the house and limped into the kitchen. While my mother started to cook I plunged into bread and butter; but before my appetite was appeased, or the steak fried, I was sound asleep. In vain my mother strove to shake me awake enough to eat the meat. Failing in this, with the assistance of my father she managed to get me to my room, where I collapsed dead asleep on the bed. They undressed me and covered me up. In the morning came the agony of being awakened. I was terribly sore, and worst of all my wrists were swelling. But I made up for my lost supper, eating an enormous breakfast, and when I hobbled to catch my car I carried a lunch twice as big as the one the day before.

Work! Let any youth just turned eighteen try to out-shovel two man-grown coal-shovelers. Work!

Long before midday I had eaten the last scrap of
my huge lunch. But I was resolved to show them
what a husky young fellow determined to rise
could do. The worst of it was that my wrists were
swelling and going back on me. There are few
who do not know the pain of walking on a sprained
ankle. Then imagine the pain of shoveling coal
and trundling a loaded wheelbarrow with two
sprained wrists.

Work! More than once I sank down on the coal
where no one could see me, and cried with rage
and mortification, and exhaustion, and despair.
That second day was my hardest, and all that
enabled me to survive it and get in the last of the
night coal at the end of thirteen hours was the
day fireman, who bound both my wrists with
broad leather straps. So tightly were they buckled
that they were like slightly flexible plaster casts.
They took the stresses and pressures which thith-
erto had been borne by my wrists, and they were
so tight that there was no room for the inflamma-
tion to rise in the sprains.

And in this fashion I continued to learn to be an
electrician. Night after night I limped home, fell
asleep before I could eat my supper, and was
helped into bed and undressed. Morning after
morning, always with huger lunches in my dinner
pail, I limped out of the house on my way to
work.

I no longer read my library books. I made no
dates with girls. I was a proper work-beast. I
worked, and ate, and slept, while my mind slept
all the time. The whole thing was a nightmare. I
worked every day, including Sunday, and I looked
far ahead to my one day off at the end of a
month, resolved to lie abed all that day and just
sleep and rest up.

The strangest part of this experience was that I
never took a drink nor thought of taking a drink.

Yet I knew that men under hard pressure almost invariably drank. I had seen them do it, and in the past had often done it myself. But so sheerly non-alcoholic was I that it never entered my mind that a drink might be good for me. I instance this to show how entirely lacking from my make-up was any predisposition toward alcohol. And the point of this instance is that later on, after more years had passed, contact with John Barleycorn at last did induce in me the alcoholic desire.

I had often noticed the day fireman staring at me in a curious way. At last, one day, he spoke. He began by swearing me to secrecy. He had been warned by the superintendent not to tell me, and in telling me he was risking his job. He told me of the day coal-passer and the night coal-passer, and of the wages they had received. I was doing for thirty dollars a month what they had received eighty dollars for doing. He would have told me sooner, the fireman said, had he not been so certain that I would break down under the work and quit. As it was, I was killing myself, and all to no good purpose. I was merely cheapening the price of labor, he argued, and keeping two men out of a job.

Being an American boy, and a proud American boy, I did not immediately quit. This was foolish of me, I know; but I resolved to continue the work long enough to prove to the superintendent that I could do it without breaking down. Then I would quit, and he would realize what a fine young fellow he had lost.

All of which I faithfully and foolishly did. I worked on until the time came when I got in the last of the night coal by six o'clock. Then I quit the job of learning electricity by doing more than two men's work for a boy's wages, went home, and proceeded to sleep the clock around.

Fortunately, I had not stayed by the job long

enough to injure myself—though I was compelled
to wear straps on my wrists for a year afterward.
But the effect of this work orgy in which I had
indulged was to sicken me with work. I just would
n't work. The thought of work was repulsive. I
did n't care if I never settled down. Learning a
trade could go hang. It was a whole lot better to
royster and frolic over the world in the way I had
previously done. So I headed out on the adventure-
path again, starting to tramp East by beating my
way on the railroads.

Chapter XXI

BUT BEHOLD! As soon as I went out on the adventure-path I met John Barleycorn again. I moved through a world of strangers, and the act of drinking together made one acquainted with men and opened the way to adventures. It might be in a saloon with jingled townsmen, or with a genial railroad man well lighted up and armed with pocket flasks, or with a bunch of alki-stiffs in a hang-out. Yes; and it might be in a prohibition state, such as Iowa was in 1894, when I wandered up the main street of Des Moines and was variously invited by strangers into various blind pigs—I remember drinking in barber-shops, plumbing establishments, and furniture stores.

Always it was John Barleycorn. Even a tramp, in those halcyon days, could get most frequently drunk. I remember, inside the prison at Buffalo, how some of us got magnificently jingled, and how on the streets of Buffalo after our release, another jingle was financed with pennies begged on the main-drag.

I had no call for alcohol, but when I was with those who drank I drank with them. I insisted on traveling or loafing with the livest, keenest men, and it was just these live, keen ones that did most of the drinking. They were the more comradely men, the more venturous, the more individual. Perhaps it was too much temperament that made them turn from the commonplace and humdrum to find relief in the lying and fantastic sureties of John Barleycorn. Be that as it may, the men I liked best, desired most to be with, were invariably to be found in John Barleycorn's company.

In the course of my tramping over the United States I achieved a new concept. As a tramp, I was behind the scenes of society—ay, and down in the cellar. I could watch the machinery work. I saw the wheels of the social machine go around, and I learned that the dignity of manual labor was n't what I had been told it was by the teachers, preachers, and politicians. The men without trades were helpless cattle. If one learned a trade, he was compelled to belong to a union in order to work at his trade. And his union was compelled to bully and slug the employers' union in order to hold up wages or hold down hours. The employ-ers' unions likewise bullied and slugged. I could n't see any dignity at all. And when a workman got old, or had an accident, he was thrown into the scrap-heap like any worn-out machine. I saw too many of this sort who were making anything but dignified ends of life.

So my new concept was that manual labor was undignified, and that it did n't pay. No trade for me, was my decision, and no superintendent's daughter. And no criminality, I also decided. That would be almost as disastrous as to be a laborer. Brains paid, not brawn, and I resolved never again to offer my muscles for sale in the brawn market. Brain, and brain only, would I sell.

I returned to California with the firm intention of developing my brain. This meant school educa-tion. I had gone through the grammar school long ago, so I entered the Oakland High School. To pay my way, I worked as a janitor. My sister helped me, too; and I was not above mowing anybody's lawn or taking up and beating carpets when I had half a day to spare. I was working to get away from work, and I buckled down to it with a grim realization of the paradox.

Boy and girl love was left behind, and along with it, Haydee and Louis Shattuck, and the early evening strolls. I had n't the time. I joined the Henry Clay Debating Society. I was received into the homes of some of the members, where I met nice girls whose skirts reached the ground. I dallied with little home clubs wherein we discussed poetry and art and the nuances of grammar. I joined the socialist local, where we studied and orated political economy, philosophy, and politics. I kept half-a-dozen membership cards working in the free library and did an immense amount of collateral reading.

And for a year and a half on end I never took a drink nor thought of taking a drink. I had n't the time, and I certainly did not have the inclination. Between my janitor-work, my studies, and innocent amusements such as chess, I had n't a moment to spare. I was discovering a new world, and such was the passion of my exploration that the old world of John Barleycorn held no inducements for me.

Come to think of it, I did enter a saloon. I went to see Johnny Heinhold in the Last Chance, and I went to borrow money. And right here is another phase of John Barleycorn. Saloon-keepers are notoriously good fellows. On an average they perform vastly greater generosities than do business men. When I simply had to have ten dollars, desperate, with no place to turn, I went to Johnny Heinhold. Several years had passed since I had been in his place or spent a cent across his bar. And when I went to borrow the ten dollars I did n't buy a drink, either. And Johnny Heinhold let me have the ten dollars, without security or interest.

More than once, in the brief days of my struggle for an education, I went to Johnny Heinhold to borrow money. When I entered the university, I borrowed forty dollars from him, without interest, without security, without buying a drink. And yet—and here is the point, the custom and the code—in the days of my prosperity, after the lapse of years, I have gone out of my way by many a long block to spend across Johnny Heinhold's bar deferred interest on the various loans. Not that Johnny Heinhold asked me to do it or expected me to do it. I did it, as I have said, in obedience to the code I had learned along with all the other things connected with John Barleycorn. In distress, when a man has no other place to turn, when he has n't the slightest bit of security which a savage-hearted pawnbroker would consider, he can go to some saloon keeper he knows. Gratitude is inherently human. When the man so helped has money again, depend upon it that a portion will be spent across the bar of the saloon keeper who befriended him.

Why, I recollect the early days of my writing career, when the small sums of money I earned from the magazines came with tragic irregularity, while at the same time I was staggering along with a growing family—a wife, children, a mother, a nephew, and my Mammy Jennie and her old husband fallen on evil days. There were two places at which I could borrow money; a barber shop and a saloon. The barber charged me five per cent. per month in advance. That is to say, when I borrowed one hundred dollars, he handed me ninety-five. The other five dollars he retained as advance interest for the first month. And on the second month I paid him five dollars more, and continued so to do each month until I made a ten-strike with the editors and lifted the loan.

The other place to which I came in trouble was the saloon. This saloon keeper I had known by sight for a couple of years. I had never spent my money in his saloon, and even when I borrowed from him I did n't spend any money. Yet never did he refuse me any sum I asked of him. Unfortunately, before I became prosperous, he moved away to another city. And to this day I regret that he is gone. It is the code I have learned. The right thing to do, and the thing I'd do right now did I know where he is, would be to drop in on occasion and spend a few dollars across his bar for old time's sake and gratitude.

This is not to exalt saloon keepers. I have written it to exalt the power of John Barleycorn, and to illustrate one more of the myriad ways by which a man is brought in contact with John Barleycorn, until in the end he finds he cannot get along without him.

But to return to the run of my narrative. Away from the adventure-path, up to my ears in study, every moment occupied, I lived oblivious to John Barleycorn's existence. Nobody about me drank. If any had drunk, and had they offered it to me, I surely would have drunk. As it was, when I had spare moments I spent them playing chess, or going with nice girls who were themselves students, or in riding a bicycle whenever I was fortunate enough to have it out of the pawnbroker's possession.

What I am insisting upon all the time is this: in me was not the slightest trace of alcoholic desire, and this despite the long and severe apprenticeship I had served under John Barleycorn. I had come back from the other side of life to be delighted with this Arcadian simplicity of student youths and student maidens. Also, I had found my way into the realm of the mind, and I was intellectually intoxicated. Alas! as I was to learn at a later period, intellectual intoxication, too, has its katzenjammer.

Chapter XXII

THREE YEARS was the time required to go through high school. I grew impatient. Also, my schooling was becoming financially impossible. At such rate I could not last out, and I did greatly want to go to the state university. When I had done a year of high school, I decided to attempt a short cut. I borrowed the money and paid to enter the senior class of a "cramming joint" or academy. I was scheduled to graduate right into the university at the end of four months, thus saving two years.

And how I did cram! I had two years' new work to do in a third of a year. For five weeks I crammed, until simultaneous quadratic equations and chemical formulas fairly oozed from my ears. And then the master of the academy took me aside. He was very sorry, but he was compelled to give me back my tuition fee and ask me to leave the school. It was n't a matter of scholarship. I stood well in my class, and did he graduate me into the university he was confident that in that institution I would continue to stand well. The trouble was that tongues were gossiping about my case. What! In four months accomplish two years' work! It would be a scandal, and the universities were becoming severer in their treatment of accredited prep schools. He could n't afford such a scandal, therefore I must gracefully depart.

I did. And I paid back the borrowed money, and gritted my teeth, and started to cram by myself. There were three months yet before the university entrance-examinations. Without laboratories, without coaching, sitting in my bedroom, I proceeded to compress the two years' work into three months and to keep reviewed on the previous year's work.

Nineteen hours a day I studied. For three months I kept this pace, only breaking it on several occasions. My body grew weary, my mind grew weary, but I stayed with it. My eyes grew weary and began to twitch, but they did not break down. Perhaps, toward the last, I got a bit dotty. I know that at the time I was confident I had discovered the formula for squaring the circle; but I resolutely deferred the working of it out until after the examinations. Then I would show them.

Came the several days of the examinations, during which time I scarcely closed my eyes in sleep, devoting every moment to cramming and reviewing. And when I turned in my last examination paper I was in full possession of a splendid case of brain-fag. I didn't want to see a book. I didn't want to think nor to lay eyes on anybody who was liable to think.

There was but one prescription for such a condition, and I gave it to myself—the adventure-path. I did n't wait to learn the result of my examinations. I stowed a roll of blankets and some cold food into a borrowed whitehall boat and set sail. Out of the Oakland Estuary I drifted on the last of an early morning ebb, caught the first of the flood up bay, and raced along with a spanking breeze. San Pablo Bay was smoking, and the Carquinez Straits off the Selby Smelter were smoking, as I picked up ahead and left astern the old landmarks I had first learned with Nelson in the unreefed *Reindeer*.

Benicia showed before me. I opened the bight of Turner's Shipyard, rounded the *Solano* wharf, and surged along abreast of the patch of tules and the clustering fishermen's-arks where in the old days I had lived and drunk deep.

And right here something happened to me, the gravity of which I never dreamed for many a long year to come. I had no intention of stopping at Benicia. The tide favored, the wind was fair and howling—glorious sailing for a sailor. Bull Head and Army Points showed ahead, marking the entrance to Suisun Bay, which I know was smoking. And yet, when I laid eyes on those fishing-arks lying in the water-front tules, without debate, on the instant, I put down my tiller, came in on the sheet, and headed for the shore. On the instant, out of the profound of my brain-fag, I knew what I wanted. I wanted to drink. I wanted to get drunk.

The call was imperative. There was no uncertainty about it. More than anything else in the world, my frayed and frazzled mind wanted surcease from weariness in the way it knew surcease would come. And right here is the point. For the first time in my life I consciously, deliberately desired to get drunk. It was a new, totally different manifestation of John Barleycorn's power. It was not a body need for alcohol. It was a mental desire. My overworked and jaded mind wanted to forget.

And here the point is drawn to its sharpest. Granted my prodigious brain-fag, nevertheless, had I never drunk in the past, the thought would never have entered my mind to get drunk now. Beginning with physical intolerance for alcohol, for years drinking only for the sake of comradeship and because alcohol was everywhere on the adventure-path, I had now reached the stage where my brain cried out, not merely for a drink, but for a drunk. And had I not been so long used to alcohol, my brain would not have so cried out. I should have sailed on past Bull Head, and in the smoking white of Suisun Bay, and in the wine of wind that filled my sail and poured through me, I should have forgotten my weary brain and rested and refreshed it.

So I sailed in to shore, made all fast, and hurried up among the arks. Charley Le Grant fell on my neck. His wife, Lizzie, folded me to her capacious breast. Billy Murphy, and Joe Lloyd, and all the survivors of the old guard, got around me and their arms around me. Charley seized the can and started for Jorgensen's saloon across the railroad tracks. That meant beer. I wanted whisky, so I called after him to bring a flask.

Many times that flask journeyed across the railroad tracks and back. More old friends of the old free and easy times dropped in, fishermen, Greeks, and Russians, and French. They took turns in treating, and treated all around in turn again. They came and went, but I stayed on and drank with all. I guzzled, I swilled. I ran the liquor down and joyed as the maggots mounted in my brain.

And Clam came in, Nelson's partner before me, handsome as ever, but more reckless, half insane, burning himself out with whisky. He had just had a quarrel with his partner on the sloop *Gazelle*, and knives had been drawn, and blows struck, and he was bent on maddening the fever of the memory with more whisky. And while we downed it, we remembered Nelson and that he had stretched out his great shoulders for the last long sleep in this very town of Benicia; and we wept over the memory of him, and remembered only the good things of him, and sent out the flask to be filled and drank again.

They wanted me to stay over, but through the open door I could see the brave wind on the water, and my ears were filled with the roar of it.

And while I forgot that I had plunged into the books nineteen hours a day for three solid months, Charley Le Grant shifted my outfit into a big Columbia River salmon boat. He added charcoal and a fisherman's brazier, a coffee pot and frying-pan, and the coffee and the meat, and a black bass fresh from the water that day.

They had to help me down the rickety wharf and into the salmon boat. Likewise they stretched my boom and sprit until the sail set like a board. Some feared to set the sprit; but I insisted, and Charley had no doubts. He knew me of old, and knew that I could sail as long as I could see. They cast off my painter. I put the tiller up, filled away before it, and with dizzy eyes checked and steadied the boat on her course and waved farewell.

The tide had turned, and the fierce ebb, running in the teeth of a fiercer wind, kicked up a stiff, upstanding sea. Suisun Bay was white with wrath and sea-lump. But a salmon boat can sail, and I knew how to sail a salmon boat. So I drove her into it, and through it, and across, and maundered aloud and chanted my disdain for all the books and schools. Cresting seas filled me a foot or so with water, but I laughed at it sloshing about my feet, and chanted my disdain for the wind and the water. I hailed myself a master of life, riding on the back of the unleashed elements, and John Barleycorn rode with me. Amid dissertations on mathematics and philosophy and spoutings and quotations, I sang all the old songs learned in the days when I went from the cannery to the oyster boats to be a pirate—such songs as: "Black Lulu," "Flying Cloud," "Treat My Daughter Kindi-ly," "The Boston Burglar," "Come All You Rambling Gambling Men," "I Wisht I Was a Little Bird," "Shenandoah," and "Ranzo, Boys, Ranzo."

Hours afterward, in the fires of sunset, where the Sacramento and the San Joaquin tumble their

muddy floods together, I took the New York Cut-
Off, skimmed across the smooth land-locked water past Black Diamond, on into the San Joaquin,
and on to Antioch, where, somewhat sobered and
magnificently hungry, I laid alongside a big potato sloop that had a familiar rig. Here were old
friends aboard, who fried my black bass in olive
oil. Then, too, there was a meaty fisherman's stew,
delicious with garlic, and crusty Italian bread without butter, and all washed down with pint mugs
of thick and heady claret.

My salmon boat was a-soak, but in the snug
cabin of the sloop dry blankets and a dry bunk
were mine; and we lay and smoked and yarned of
old days, while overhead the wind screamed
through the rigging and taut halyards drummed
against the mast.

Chapter XXIII

M Y CRUISE in the salmon boat lasted a week, and I returned ready to enter the university. During the week's cruise I did not drink again. To accomplish this I was compelled to avoid looking up old friends, for as ever the adventure-path was beset with John Barleycorn. I had wanted the drink that first day, and in the days that followed I did not want it. My tired brain had recuperated. I had no moral scruples in the matter. I was not ashamed nor sorry because of that first day's orgy at Benicia, and I thought no more about it, returning gladly to my books and studies.

Long years were to pass ere I looked back upon that day and realized its significance. At the time, and for a long time afterward, I was to think of it only as a frolic. But still later, in the slough of brain-fag and intellectual weariness, I was to remember and know the craving for the anodyne that resides in alcohol.

In the meantime, after this one relapse at Benicia, I went on with my abstemiousness, primarily because I did n't want to drink. And next, I was abstemious because my way led among books and students, where no drinking was. Had I been out on the adventure-path, I should as a matter of course have been drinking. For that is the pity of the adventure-path, which is one of John Barleycorn's favorite stamping-grounds.

I completed the first half of my freshman year,

and in January of 1897 took up my course for the second half. But the pressure from lack of money, plus a conviction that the university was not giving me all that I wanted in the time I could spare for it, forced me to leave. I was not very disappointed. For two years I had studied, and in those two years, what was far more valuable, I had done a prodigious amount of reading. Then, too, my grammar had improved. It is true, I had not yet learned that I must say "It is I"; but I no longer was guilty of the double negative in writing, though still prone to that error in excited speech.

I decided immediately to embark on my career. I had four preferences: first, music; second, poetry; third, the writing of philosophic, economic, and political essays; and, fourth, and last, and least, fiction writing. I resolutely cut out music as impossible, settled down in my bedroom, and tackled my second, third and fourth choices simultaneously. Heavens, how I wrote! Never was there a creative fever such as mine from which the patient escaped fatal results. The way I worked was enough to soften my brain and send me to a mad-house. I wrote, I wrote everything—ponderous essays, scientific and sociological, short stories, humorous verse, verse of all sorts from triolets and sonnets to blank verse tragedy and elephantine epics in Spenserian stanzas. On occasion I composed steadily, day after day, for fifteen hours a day. At times I forgot to eat, or refused to tear myself away from my passionate outpouring in order to eat.

And then there was the matter of typewriting. My brother-in-law owned a machine which he used in the daytime. In the night I was free to use it. That machine was a wonder. I could weep now as I recollect my wrestlings with it. It must have been a first model in the year one of the type-

writer era. Its alphabet was all capitals. It was
informed with an evil spirit. It obeyed no known
laws of physics, and overthrew the hoary axiom
that like things performed to like things produce
like results. I 'll swear that machine never did the
same thing in the same way twice. Again and
again, it demonstrated that unlike actions produce
like results.

How my back used to ache with it! Prior to that
experience, my back had been good for every
violent strain put upon it in a none too gentle
career. But that typewriter proved to me that I
had a pipe-stem for a back. Also, it made me
doubt my shoulders. They ached as with rheuma-
tism after every bout. The keys of that machine
had to be hit so hard that to one outside the
house it sounded like distant thunder or some
one breaking up the furniture. I had to hit the
keys so hard that I strained my first fingers to the
elbows, while the ends of my fingers were blisters
burst and blistered again. Had it been my machine I 'd have operated it with a carpenter's
hammer.

The worst of it was that I was actually typing
my manuscripts at the same time I was trying to
master that machine. It was a feat of physical
endurance and a brain storm combined to type a
thousand words, and I was composing thousands
of words every day which just had to be typed for
the waiting editors.

Oh, between the writing and the typewriting I
was well a-weary. I had brain- and nerve-fag, and
body-fag as well, and yet the thought of drink
never suggested itself. I was living too high to
stand in need of an anodyne. All my waking
hours, except those with that infernal typewriter,
were spent in a creative heaven. And along with
this I had no desire for drink, because I still believed in many things—in the love of all men and

women in the matter of man and woman love; in fatherhood; in human justice; in art—in the whole host of fond illusions that keep the world turning around.

But the waiting editors elected to keep on waiting. My manuscripts made amazing round-trip records between the Pacific and the Atlantic. It might have been the weirdness of the typewriting that prevented the editors from accepting at least one little offering of mine. I don't know, and goodness knows the stuff I wrote was as weird as its typing. I sold my hard-bought school books for ridiculous sums to second-hand bookmen. I borrowed small sums of money wherever I could, and suffered my old father to feed me with the meager returns of his failing strength.

It did n't last long, only a few weeks, when I had to surrender and go to work. Yet I was unaware of any need for the drink-anodyne. I was not disappointed. My career was retarded, that was all. Perhaps I did need further preparation. I had learned enough from the books to realize that I had touched only the hem of knowledge's garment. I still lived on the heights. My waking hours, and most of the hours I should have used for sleep, were spent with the books.

Chapter XXIV

OUT IN THE COUNTRY, at the Belmont Academy, I went to work in a small, perfectly appointed steam laundry. Another fellow and myself did all the work from sorting and washing to ironing the white shirts, collars and cuffs, and the "fancy starch" of the wives of the professors. We worked like tigers, especially as summer came on and the academy boys took to the wearing of duck trousers. It consumes a dreadful lot of time to iron one pair of duck trousers. And there were so many pairs of them. We sweated our way through long sizzling weeks at a task that was never done; and many a night, while the students snored in bed, my partner and I toiled on under the electric light at steam mangle or ironing board.

The hours were long, the work was arduous, despite the fact that we became past masters in the art of eliminating waste motion. And I was receiving thirty dollars a month and board—a slight increase over my coal-shoveling and cannery days, at least to the extent of board, which cost my employer little (we ate in the kitchen), but which was to me the equivalent of twenty dollars a month. My robuster strength of added years, my increased skill, and all I had learned from the books, were responsible for this increase of twenty dollars. Judging by my rate of development, I might hope before I died to be a night watchman for sixty dollars a month, or a policeman actually receiving a hundred dollars with pickings.

So relentlessly did my partner and I spring into our work throughout the week that by Saturday night we were frazzled wrecks. I found myself in the old familiar work-beast condition, toiling longer hours than the horses toiled, thinking scarcely more frequent thoughts than horses think. The books were closed to me. I had brought a trunkful to the laundry, but found myself unable to read them. I fell asleep the moment I tried to read; and if I did manage to keep my eyes open for several pages, I could not remember the contents of those pages. I gave over attempts on heavy study, such as jurisprudence, political economy, and biology, and tried lighter stuff, such as history. I fell asleep. I tried literature, and fell asleep. And finally, when I fell asleep over lively novels, I gave up. I never succeeded in reading one book in all the time I spent in the laundry.

And when Saturday night came, and the week's work was over until Monday morning, I knew only one desire besides the desire to sleep, and that was to get drunk. This was the second time in my life that I had heard the unmistakable call of John Barleycorn. The first time it had been because of brain-fag. But I had no overworked brain now. On the contrary, all I knew was the dull numbness of a brain that was not worked at all. That was the trouble. My brain had become so alert and eager, so quickened by the wonder of the new world the books had discovered to it, that it now suffered all the misery of stagnancy and inaction.

And I, the long-time intimate of John Barleycorn, knew just what he promised me—maggots of fancy, dreams of power, forgetfulness, anything and everything save whirling washers, revolving mangles, humming centrifugal wringers, and fancy starch and interminable processions of duck trousers moving in steam under my flying iron. And that 's it. John Barleycorn makes his appeal to weakness and failure, to weariness and exhaustion. He is the easy way out. And he is lying all the time. He offers false strength to the body, false elevation to the spirit, making things seem what they are not and vastly fairer than what they are.

But it must not be forgotten that John Barleycorn is protean. As well as to weakness and exhaustion, does he appeal to too much strength, to superabundant vitality, to the ennui of idleness. He can tuck in his arm the arm of any man in any mood. He can throw the net of his lure over all men. He exchanges new lamps for old, the spangles of illusion for the drabs of reality, and in the end cheats all who traffic with him.

I did n't get drunk, however, for the simple reason that it was a mile and a half to the nearest saloon. And this, in turn, was because the call to get drunk was not very loud in my ears. Had it been loud, I would have traveled ten times the distance to win to the saloon. On the other hand, had the saloon been just around the corner, I should have got drunk. As it was, I would sprawl out in the shade on my one day of rest and dally with the Sunday papers. But I was too weary even for their froth. The comic supplement might bring a pallid smile to my face, and then I would fall asleep.

Although I did not yield to John Barleycorn while working in the laundry, a certain definite result was produced. I had heard the call, felt the gnaw of desire, yearned for the anodyne. I was being prepared for the stronger desire of later years.

And the point is that this development of desire was entirely in my brain. My body did not cry out for alcohol. As always, alcohol was repulsive to my body. When I was bodily weary from shoveling coal, the thought of taking a drink had never flickered into my consciousness. When I was brain-wearied after taking the entrance examinations to the university, I promptly got drunk. At the laundry, I was suffering physical exhaustion again, and physical exhaustion that was not nearly as profound as that of the coal-shoveling. But there was a difference. When I went coal-shoveling, my mind had not yet awakened. Between that time and the laundry my mind had found the kingdom of the mind. While shoveling coal, my mind was somnolent. While toiling in the laundry, my mind, informed and eager to do and be, was crucified.

And whether I yielded to drink, as at Benicia, or whether I refrained, as at the laundry, in my brain the seeds of desire for alcohol were germinating.

Chapter XXV

AFTER THE LAUNDRY, my sister and her husband grubstaked me into the Klondike. It was the first gold rush into that region, the early fall rush of 1897. I was twenty-one years old, and in splendid physical condition. I remember, at the end of the twenty-eight-mile portage across Chilkoot from Dyea Beach to Lake Linderman, I was packing up with the Indians and outpacking many an Indian. The last pack into Linderman was three miles. I back-tripped it four times a day, and on each forward trip carried one hundred and fifty pounds. This means that over the worst trails I daily traveled twenty-four miles, twelve of which were under a burden of one hundred and fifty pounds.

Yes, I had let career go hang, and was on the adventure-path again in quest of fortune. And of course, on the adventure-path, I met John Barleycorn. Here were the chesty men again, rovers and adventurers, and while they did n't mind a grub famine, whisky they could not do without. Whisky went over the trail, while the flour lay cached and untouched by the trail-side.

As good fortune would have it, the three men in my party were not drinkers. Therefore I did n't drink save on rare occasions and disgracefully when with other men. In my personal medicine chest was a quart of whisky. I never drew the cork till six months afterwards, in a lonely camp, where, without anesthetics, a doctor was compelled to operate on a man. The doctor and the patient emptied my bottle between them and then proceeded to the operation.

Back in California a year later, recovering from scurvy, I found that my father was dead and that I was the head and the sole bread-winner of a household. When I state that I had passed coal on a steamship from Behring Sea to British Columbia, and traveled in the steerage from there to San Francisco, it will be understood that I brought nothing back from the Klondike but my scurvy.

Times were hard. Work of any sort was difficult to get. And work of any sort was what I had to take, for I was still an unskilled laborer. I had no thought of career. That was over and done with. I had to find food for two mouths beside my own and keep a roof over our heads—yes, and buy a winter suit, my one suit being decidedly summery. I had to get some sort of work immediately. After that, when I had caught my breath, I might think about my future.

Unskilled labor is the first to feel the slackness of hard times, and I had no trades save those of sailor and laundryman. With my new responsibilities I did n't dare go to sea, and I failed to find a job at laundrying. I failed to find a job at anything. I had my name down in five employment bureaus. I advertised in three newspapers. I sought out the few friends I knew who might be able to get me work; but they were either uninterested or unable to find anything for me.

The situation was desperate. I pawned my watch, my bicycle, and a mackintosh of which my father had been very proud and which he had left to me. It was and is my sole legacy in this world. It had cost fifteen dollars, and the pawnbroker let me have two dollars on it. And—oh, yes—a waterfront comrade of earlier years drifted along one day with a dress suit wrapped in newspapers.

He could give no adequate explanation of how he had come to possess it, nor did I press for an explanation. I wanted the suit myself. No; not to wear. I traded him a lot of rubbish which, being unpawnable, was useless to me. He peddled the rubbish for several dollars, while I pledged the dress suit with my pawnbroker for five dollars. And for all I know, the pawnbroker still has the suit. I had never intended to redeem it.

But I could n't get any work. Yet I was a bargain in the labor market. I was twenty-two years old, weighed one hundred and sixty-five pounds stripped, every pound of which was excellent for toil; and the last traces of my scurvy were vanishing before a treatment of potatoes chewed raw. I tackled every opening for employment. I tried to become a studio model, but there were too many fine-bodied young fellows out of jobs. I answered advertisements of elderly invalids in need of companions. And I almost became a sewing machine agent, on commission, without salary. But poor people don't buy sewing machines in hard times, so I was forced to forego that employment.

Of course, it must be remembered that along with such frivolous occupations, I was trying to get work as wop, lumper, and roustabout. But winter was coming on, and the surplus labor army was pouring into the cities. Also, I, who had romped along carelessly through the countries of the world and the kingdom of the mind, was not a member of any union.

I sought odd jobs. I worked days, and half-days, at anything I could get. I mowed lawns, trimmed hedges, took up carpets, beat them, and laid them again. Further, I took the civil service examinations for mail carrier and passed first. But alas, there was no vacancy, and I must wait. And while I waited, and in between the odd jobs I managed to procure, I started to earn ten dollars by writing a newspaper account of a voyage I had made, in an open boat down the Yukon, of nineteen hundred miles in nineteen days. I did n't know the first thing about the newspaper game, but I was confident I 'd get ten dollars for my article.

But I did n't. The first San Francisco newspaper to which I mailed it never acknowledged receipt of the manuscript, but held on to it. The longer it held on to it, the more certain I was that the thing was accepted.

And here is the funny thing. Some are born to fortune, and some have fortune thrust upon them. But in my case I was clubbed into fortune, and bitter necessity wielded the club. I had long since abandoned all thought of writing as a career. My honest intention in writing that article was to earn ten dollars. And that was the limit of my intention. It would help to tide me along until I got steady employment. Had a vacancy occurred in the post office at that time, I should have jumped at it.

But the vacancy did not occur, nor did a steady job; and I employed the time between odd jobs with writing a twenty-one-thousand-word serial for the "Youth's Companion." I turned it out and typed it in seven days. I fancy that was what was the matter with it, for it came back.

It took some time for it to go and come, and in the meantime I tried my hand at short stories. I sold one to the *Overland Monthly* for five dollars. The *Black Cat* gave me forty dollars for another. The *Overland Monthly* offered me seven dollars and a half, pay on publication, for all the stories I should deliver. I got my bicycle, my watch, and my father's mackintosh out of pawn and rented a typewriter. Also, I paid up the bills I owed to the several groceries that allowed me a small credit. I recall the Portuguese groceryman who never permitted my bill to go beyond four dollars. Hopkins, another grocer, could not be budged beyond five dollars.

And just then came the call from the post office to go to work. It placed me in a most trying predicament. The sixty-five dollars I could earn regularly every month was a terrible temptation. I could n't decide what to do. And I 'll never be able to forgive the postmaster of Oakland. I answered the call, and I talked to him like a man. I frankly told him the situation. It looked as if I might win out at writing. The chance was good, but not certain. Now, if he would pass me by and select the next man on the eligible list, and give me a call at the next vacancy—

But he shut me off with: "Then you don't want the position?"

"But I do," I protested. "Don't you see, if you will pass me over this time—"

"If you want it you will take it," he said coldly.

Happily for me, the cursed brutality of the man made me angry.

"Very well," I said. "I won't take it."

Chapter XXVI

HAVING BURNED my one ship, I plunged into writing. I am afraid I always was an extremist. Early and late I was at it—writing, typing, studying grammar, studying writing and all the forms of writing, and studying the writers who succeeded in order to find out how they succeeded. I managed on five hours' sleep in the twenty-four, and came pretty close to working the nineteen waking hours left to me. My light burned till two and three in the morning, which led a good neighbor woman into a bit of sentimental Sherlock Holmes deduction. Never seeing me in the daytime, she concluded that I was a gambler, and that the light in my window was placed there by my mother to guide her erring son home.

The trouble with the beginner at the writing game is the long, dry spells, when there is never an editor's check and everything pawnable is pawned. I wore my summer suit pretty well through that winter, and the following summer experienced the longest, dryest spell of all, in the period when salaried men are gone on vacation and manuscripts lie in editorial offices until vacation is over.

My difficulty was that I had no one to advise me. I did n't know a soul who had written or who had ever tried to write. I did n't even know one reporter. Also, to succeed at the writing game, I found I had to unlearn about everything the teachers and professors of literature of the high school and university had taught me. I was very indignant about this at the time; though now I can understand it. They did not know the trick of successful writing in the years of 1895 and 1896. They knew all about "Snow Bound" and "Sartor Resartus"; but the American editors of 1899 did not want such truck. They wanted the 1899 truck, and offered to pay so well for it that the teachers and professors of literature would have quit their jobs could they have supplied it.

I struggled along, stood off the butcher and the grocer, pawned my watch and bicycle and my father's mackintosh, and I worked. I really did work, and went on short commons of sleep. Critics have complained about the swift education one of my characters, Martin Eden, achieved. In three years, from a sailor with a common school education, I made a successful writer of him. The critics say this is impossible. Yet I was Martin Eden. At the end of three working years, two of which were spent in high school and the university and one spent at writing, and all three in studying immensely and intensely, I was publishing stories in magazines such as the _Atlantic Monthly_, was correcting proofs of my first book (issued by Houghton, Mifflin Co.), was selling sociological articles to _Cosmopolitan_ and _McClure's_, had declined an associate editorship proffered me by telegraph from New York City, and was getting ready to marry.

Now the foregoing means work, especially the last year of it, when I was learning my trade as a writer. And in that year, running short on sleep and tasking my brain to its limit, I neither drank nor cared to drink. So far as I was concerned, alcohol did not exist. I did suffer from brain-fag on occasion, but alcohol never suggested itself as an ameliorative. Heavens! Editorial acceptances and

checks were all the amelioratives I needed. A thin
envelope from an editor in the morning's mail
was more stimulating than half-a-dozen cocktails.
And if a check of decent amount came out of the
envelope, such incident in itself was a whole drunk.

Furthermore, at that time in my life I did not
know what a cocktail was. I remember, when my
first book was published, several Alaskans who
were members of the Bohemian Club entertained
me one evening at the club in San Francisco. We
sat in most wonderful leather chairs, and drinks
were ordered. Never had I heard such an ordering of liqueurs and of highballs of particular brands
of Scotch. I did n't know what a liqueur or a highball was, and I did n't know that "Scotch" meant
whisky. I knew only poor men's drinks, the drinks
of the frontier and of a sailor-town—cheap beer
and cheaper whisky that was just called whisky
and nothing else. I was embarrassed to make a
choice, and the waiter nearly collapsed when I
ordered claret as an after-dinner drink.

Chapter XXVII

As I SUCCEEDED with my writing, my standard of living rose and my horizon broadened. I confined myself to writing and typing a thousand words a day, including Sundays and holidays; and I still studied hard, but not so hard as formerly. I allowed myself five and one-half hours of actual sleep. I added this half-hour because I was compelled. Financial success permitted me more time for exercise. I rode my wheel more, chiefly because it was permanently out of pawn; and I boxed and fenced, walked on my hands, jumped high and broad, put the shot and tossed the caber, and went swimming. And I learned that more sleep is required for physical exercise than for mental exercise. There were tired nights, bodily, when I slept six hours; and on occasion of very severe exercise I actually slept seven hours. But such sleep orgies were not frequent. There was so much to learn, so much to be done, that I felt wicked when I slept seven hours. And I blessed the man who invented alarm clocks.

And still no desire to drink. I possessed too many fine faiths, was living at too keen a pitch. I was a socialist, intent on saving the world, and alcohol could not give me the fervors that were mine from ideas and ideals. My voice, on account of my successful writing, had added weight, or so I thought. At any rate, my reputation as a writer drew me audiences that my reputation as a speaker never could have drawn. I was invited before clubs and organizations of all sorts to deliver my message. I fought the good fight, and went on studying and writing, and was very busy.

Up to this time I had had a very restricted circle of friends. But now I began to go about. I was invited out, especially to dinner; and I made many friends and acquaintances whose economic lives were easier than mine had been. And many of them drank. In their own houses they drank and offered me drink. They were not drunkards any of them. They just drank temperately, and I drank temperately with them as an act of comradeship and accepted hospitality. I did not care for it, neither wanted it nor did not want it, and so small was the impression made by it that I do not remember my first cocktail nor my first Scotch highball.

Well, I had a house. When one is asked into other houses, he naturally asks others into his house. Behold the rising standard of living. Having been given drink in other houses, I could expect nothing else of myself than to give drink in my own house. So I laid in a supply of beer and whisky and table claret. Never since that has my house not been well supplied.

And still, through all this period, I did not care in the slightest for John Barleycorn. I drank when others drank, and with them, as a social act. And I had so little choice in the matter that I drank whatever they drank. If they elected whisky, then whisky it was for me. If they drank root beer or sarsaparilla, I drank root beer or sarsaparilla with them. And when there were no friends in the house, why, I did n't drink anything. Whisky decanters were always in the room where I wrote, and for months and years I never knew what it was, when by myself, to take a drink.

When out at dinner, I noticed the kindly, genial

glow of the preliminary cocktail. It seemed a very
fitting and gracious thing. Yet so little did I stand in
need of it, with my own high intensity and vitality, that I never thought it worth while to have a
cocktail before my own meal when I ate alone.

On the other hand, I well remember a very
brilliant man, somewhat older than I, who occasionally visited me. He liked whisky, and I recall
sitting whole afternoons in my den, drinking steadily with him, drink for drink, until he was mildly
lighted up and I was slightly aware that I had
drunk some whisky. Now why did I do that? I
don't know, save that the old schooling held, the
training of the old days and nights, glass in hand,
with men, the drinking ways of drink and drinkers.

Besides, I no longer feared John Barleycorn.
Mine was that most dangerous stage when a man
believes himself John Barleycorn's master. I had
proved it to my satisfaction in the long years of
work and study. I could drink when I wanted,
refrain when I wanted, drink without getting
drunk, and to cap everything I was thoroughly
conscious that I had no liking for the stuff. During
this period I drank precisely for the same reason I
had drunk with Scotty and the harpooner and
with the oyster pirates—because it was an act
performed by men with whom I wanted to behave as a man. These brilliant ones, these adventurers of the mind, drank. Very well. There was
no reason I should not drink with them,—I who
knew so confidently that I had nothing to fear
from John Barleycorn.

And the foregoing was my attitude of mind for
years. Occasionally I got well jingled, but such
occasions were rare. It interfered with my work,
and I permitted nothing to interfere with my work.
I remember, when spending several months in
the East End of London, during which time I
wrote a book and adventured much amongst the

worst of the slum classes, that I got drunk several times and was mightily wroth with myself because it interfered with my writing. Yet these very times were because I was out on the adventure-path, where John Barleycorn is always to be found.

Then, too, with the certitude of long training and unholy intimacy, there were occasions when I engaged in drinking-bouts with men. Of course, this was on the adventure-path in various parts of the world, and it was a matter of pride. It is a queer man-pride that leads one to drink with men in order to show as strong a head as they. But this queer man-pride is no theory. It is a fact.

For instance, a wild band of young revolutionists invited me as the guest of honor to a beer bust. It is the only technical beer bust I ever attended. I did not know the true inwardness of the affair when I accepted. I imagined that the talk would be wild and high, that some of them might drink more than they ought, and that I would drink discreetly. But it seemed these beer busts were a diversion of these high-spirited young fellows whereby they whiled away the tedium of existence by making fools of their betters. As I learned afterward, they had got their previous guest of honor, a brilliant young radical, unskilled in drinking, quite pipped.

When I found myself with them, and the situation dawned on me, up rose my queer man-pride. I'd show them, the young rascals. I'd show them who was husky and chesty, who had the vitality and the constitution, the stomach and the head, who could make most of a swine of himself and show it least. These unlicked cubs who thought they could out-drink *me*!

You see, it was an endurance test, and no man likes to give another best. Faugh! It was steam beer. I had learned more expensive brews. Not for years had I drunk steam beer; but when I had, I

had drunk with men, and I guessed I could show
these youngsters some ability in beer-guzzling.
And the drinking began, and I had to drink with
the best of them. Some of them might lag, but the
guest of honor was not permitted to lag.

And all my austere nights of midnight oil, all
the books I had read, all the wisdom I had gathered, went glimmering before the ape and tiger in
me that crawled up from the abysm of my hered-
ity, atavistic, competitive and brutal, lustful with
strength and desire to outswine the swine.

And when the session broke up I was still on
my feet, and I walked erect, unswaying—which
was more than can be said of some of my hosts. I
recall one of them in indignant tears on the street
corner, weeping as he pointed out my sober condition. Little he dreamed the iron clutch, born of
old training, with which I held to my consciousness in my swimming brain, kept control of my
muscles and my qualms, kept my voice unbroken
and easy and my thoughts consecutive and logical. Yes, and mixed up with it all I was privily
a-grin. They had n't made a fool of me in that
drinking bout. And I was proud of myself for the
achievement. Darn it, I am still proud, so strangely
is man compounded.

But I did n't write my thousand words next morning. I was sick, poisoned. It was a day of wretchedness. In the afternoon I had to give a public
speech. I gave it, and I am confident it was as bad
as I felt. Some of my hosts were there in the front
rows to mark any signs on me of the night before.
I don't known what signs they marked, but I
marked signs on them and took consolation in the
knowledge that they were just as sick as I.

Never again, I swore. And I have never been
inveigled into another beer bust. For that matter,
that was my last drinking bout of any sort. Oh, I
have drunk ever since, but with more wisdom,

more discretion, and never in a competitive spirit. It is thus the seasoned drinker grows seasoned.

To show that at this period in my life drinking was wholly a matter of companionship, I remember crossing the Atlantic in the old *Teutonic*. It chanced, at the start, that I chummed with an English cable operator and a younger member of a Spanish shipping firm. Now the only thing they drank was "horse's neck"—a long, soft, cool drink with an apple peel or an orange peel floating in it. And for that whole voyage I drank horse's necks with my two companions. On the other hand, had they drunk whisky, I should have drunk whisky with them. From this it must not be concluded that I was merely weak. I did n't care. I had no morality in the matter. I was strong with youth, and unafraid, and alcohol was an utterly negligible question so far as I was concerned.

Chapter XXVIII

NOT YET was I ready to tuck my arm in John Barleycorn's. The older I got, the greater my success, the more money I earned, the wider was the command of the world that became mine and the more prominently did John Barleycorn bulk in my life. And still I maintained no more than a nodding acquaintance with him. I drank for the sake of sociability, and when alone I did not drink. Sometimes I got jingled, but I considered such jingles the mild price I paid for sociability.

To show how unripe I was for John Barleycorn, when, at this time, I descended into my slough of despond, I never dreamed of turning to John Barleycorn for a helping hand. I had life troubles and heart troubles which are neither here nor there in this narrative. But, combined with them, were intellectual troubles which are indeed germane.

Mine was no uncommon experience. I had read too much positive science and lived too much positive life. In the eagerness of youth I had made the ancient mistake of pursuing Truth too relentlessly. I had torn her veils from her, and the sight was too terrible for me to stand. In brief, I lost my fine faiths in pretty well everything except humanity, and the humanity I retained faith in was a very stark humanity indeed.

This long sickness of pessimism is too well known to most of us to be detailed here. Let it suffice to state that I had it very bad. I meditated suicide coolly, as a Greek philosopher might. My regret was that there were too many dependent directly upon me for food and shelter for me to quit living. But that was sheer morality. What really saved me was the one remaining illusion—the PEOPLE.

The things I had fought for and burned my midnight oil for, had failed me. Success—I despised it. Recognition—it was dead ashes. Society, men and women above the ruck and the muck of the water-front and the forecastle—I was appalled by their unlovely mental mediocrity. Love of woman—it was like all the rest. Money—I could sleep in only one bed at a time, and of what worth was an income of a hundred porterhouses a day when I could eat only one? Art, culture—in the face of the iron facts of biology such things were ridiculous, the exponents of such things only the more ridiculous.

From the foregoing it can be seen how very sick I was. I was born a fighter. The things I had fought for had proved not worth the fight. Remained the PEOPLE. My fight was finished, yet something was left still to fight for—the PEOPLE.

But while I was discovering this one last tie to bind me to life, in my extremity, in the depths of despond, walking in the valley of the shadow, my ears were deaf to John Barleycorn. Never the remotest whisper arose in my consciousness that John Barleycorn was the anodyne, that he could lie me along to live. One way only was uppermost in my thought—my revolver, the crashing eternal darkness of a bullet. There was plenty of whisky in the house—for my guests. I never touched it. I grew afraid of my revolver—afraid during the period in which the radiant, flashing vision of the PEOPLE was forming in my mind and will. So obsessed was I with the desire to die, that I feared I might commit the act in my sleep, and I was compelled to give my revolver away to others who were to lose it for me where my subconscious hand might not find it.

But the PEOPLE saved me. By the PEOPLE was I handcuffed to life. There was still one fight left in me, and here was the thing for which to fight. I threw all precaution to the winds, threw myself with fiercer zeal into the fight for socialism, laughed at the editors and publishers who warned me and who were the sources of my hundred porterhouses a day, and was brutally careless of whose feelings I hurt and of how savagely I hurt them. As the "well-balanced radicals" charged at the time, my efforts were so strenuous, so unsafe and unsane, so ultra-revolutionary, that I retarded the socialist development in the United States by five years. In passing, I wish to remark, at this late date, that it is my fond belief that I accelerated the socialist development in the United States by at least five minutes.

It was the PEOPLE, and no thanks to John Barleycorn, who pulled me through my long sickness. And when I was convalescent, came the love of woman to complete the cure and lull my pessimism asleep for many a long day, until John Barleycorn again awoke it. But, in the meantime, I pursued Truth less relentlessly, refraining from tearing her last veils aside even when I clutched them in my hand. I no longer cared to look upon Truth naked. I refused to permit myself to see a second time what I had once seen. And the memory of what I had that time seen I resolutely blotted from my mind.

And I was very happy. Life went well with me. I took delight in little things. The big things I declined to take too seriously. I still read the books, but not with the old eagerness. I still read the books to-day, but never again shall I read them with that old glory of youthful passion when I harked to the call from over and beyond that whispered me on to win to the mystery at the back of life and behind the stars.

The point of this chapter is that, in the long sickness that at some time comes to most of us, I came through without any appeal for aid to John Barleycorn. Love, socialism, the PEOPLE—healthful figments of man's mind—were the things that cured and saved me. If ever a man was not a born alcoholic, I believe that I am that man. And yet . . . well, let the succeeding chapters tell their tale, for in them will be shown how I paid for my previous quarter of a century of contact with ever-accessible John Barleycorn.

Chapter XXIX

AFTER MY LONG SICKNESS my drinking continued to be convivial. I drank when others drank and I was with them. But, imperceptibly, my need for alcohol took form and began to grow. It was not a body need. I boxed, swam, sailed, rode horses, lived in the open an arrantly healthful life, and passed life insurance examinations with flying colors. In its inception, now that I look back upon it, this need for alcohol was a mental need, a nerve need, a good-spirits need. How can I explain?

It was something like this. Physiologically, from the standpoint of palate and stomach, alcohol was, as it had always been, repulsive. It tasted no better than beer did when I was five, than bitter claret did when I was seven. When I was alone, writing or studying, I had no need for it. But—I was growing old, or wise, or both, or senile as an alternative. When I was in company I was less pleased, less excited, with the things said and done. Erstwhile worth-while fun and stunts seemed no longer worth while; and it was a torment to listen to the insipidities and stupidities of women, to the pompous, arrogant sayings of the little half-baked men. It is the penalty one pays for reading the books too much, or for being oneself a fool. In my case it does not matter which was my trouble. The trouble itself was the fact. The condition of the fact was mine. For me the life, and light, and sparkle of human intercourse were dwindling.

I had climbed too high among the stars, or, maybe, I had slept too hard. Yet I was not hysterical nor in any way overwrought. My pulse was normal. My heart was an amazement of excellence to the insurance doctors. My lungs threw the said doctors into ecstasies. I wrote a thousand words every day. I was punctiliously exact in dealing with all the affairs of life that fell to my lot. I exercised in joy and gladness. I slept at night like a babe. But—

Well, as soon as I got out in the company of others I was driven to melancholy and spiritual tears. I could neither laugh with nor at the solemn utterances of men I esteemed ponderous asses; nor could I laugh with nor at, nor engage in my old-time lightsome persiflage, with the silly superficial chatterings of women, who, underneath all their silliness and softness, were as primitive, direct, and deadly in their pursuit of biological destiny as the monkey women were before they shed their furry coats and replaced them the furs of other animals.

And I was not pessimistic. I swear I was not pessimistic. I was merely bored. I had seen the same show too often, listened too often to the same songs and the same jokes. I knew too much about the box-office receipts. I knew the cogs of the machinery behind the scenes so well, that the posing on the stage, and the laughter and the song, could not drown the creaking of the wheels behind.

It does n't pay to go behind the scenes and see the angel-voiced tenor beat his wife. Well, I 'd been behind, and I was paying for it. Or else I was a fool. It is immaterial which was my situation. The situation is what counts, and the situation was that social intercourse for me was getting painful and difficult. On the other hand, it must be stated that on rare occasions, on very rare occasions, I did meet rare souls, or fools like me, with whom I could spend magnificent hours among the stars, or in the paradise of fools. I was married to a rare soul, or a fool, who never bored me and who was always a source of new and unending surprise and delight. But I could not spend all my hours solely in her company. Nor would it have been fair, nor wise, to compel her to spend all her hours in my company. Besides, I had written a string of successful books, and society demands some portion of the recreative hours of a fellow that writes books. And any normal man, of himself and his needs, demands some hours of his fellow man.

And now we begin to come to it. How to face social intercourse with the glamour gone? John Barleycorn! The ever-patient one had waited a quarter of a century and more for me to reach my hand out in need of him. His thousand tricks had failed, thanks to my constitution and good luck, but he had more tricks in his bag. A cocktail or two, or several, I found, cheered me up for the foolishness of foolish people. A cocktail or several, before dinner, enabled me to laugh wholeheartedly at things which had long since ceased being laughable. The cocktail was a prod, a spur, a kick, to my jaded mind and bored spirits. It recrudesced the laughter and the song, and put a little into my own imagination so that I could laugh and sing and say foolish things with the liveliest of them, or platitudes with verve and intensity to the satisfaction of the pompous mediocre ones who knew no other way to talk.

A poor companion without a cocktail, I became a very good companion with one. I achieved a false exhilaration, drugged myself to merriment. And the thing began so imperceptibly, that I, old intimate of John Barleycorn, never dreamed whither it was leading me. I was beginning to call for music

and wine; soon I should be calling for madder
music and more wine.

It was at this time I became aware of waiting
with expectancy for the pre-dinner cocktail. I *wanted*
it, and I was *conscious* that I wanted it. I remember, while war-corresponding in the Far East, of
being irresistibly attracted to a certain home. Besides accepting all invitations to dinner, I made a
point of dropping in almost every afternoon. Now,
the hostess was a charming woman, but it was
not for her sake that I was under her roof so
frequently. It happened that she made by far the
finest cocktail procurable in that large city where
drink-mixing on the part of the foreign population
was indeed an art. Up at the club, down at the
hotels, and in other private houses, no such cocktails were created. Her cocktails were subtle. They
were masterpieces. They were the least repulsive
to the palate and carried the most "kick." And
yet, I desired her cocktails only for sociability's
sake, to key myself to sociable moods. When I
rode away from that city, across hundreds of miles
of rice-fields and mountains, and through months
of campaigning, and on with the victorious Japanese into Manchuria, I did not drink. Several bottles of whisky were always to be found on the
backs of my pack-horses. Yet I never broached a
bottle for myself, never took a drink by myself,
and never knew a desire to take such a drink. Oh,
if a white man came into my camp, I opened a
bottle and we drank together according to the way
of men, just as he would open a bottle and drink
with me if I came into his camp. I carried that
whisky for social purposes, and I so charged it up
in my expense account to the newspaper for which
I worked.

Only in retrospect can I mark the almost imper-
ceptible growth of my desire. There were little
hints then that I did not take, little straws in the

wind that I did not see, little incidents the gravity of which I did not realize.

For instance, for some years it had been my practice each winter to cruise for six or eight weeks on San Francisco Bay. My stout sloop yacht, the *Spray*, had a comfortable cabin and a coal stove. A Korean boy did the cooking, and I usually took a friend or so along to share the joys of the cruise. Also, I took my machine along and did my thousand words a day. On the particular trip I have in mind, Cloudesley and Toddy came along. This was Toddy's first trip. On previous trips Cloudesley had elected to drink beer; so I had kept the yacht supplied with beer and had drunk beer with him.

But on this cruise the situation was different. Toddy was so nicknamed because of his diabolical cleverness in concocting toddies. So I brought whisky along—a couple of gallons. Alas! Many another gallon I bought, for Cloudesley and I got into the habit of drinking a certain hot toddy of huge dimensions that actually tasted delicious going down and that carried the most exhilarating kick imaginable.

I *liked* those toddies. I grew to look forward to the making of them. We drank them regularly, one before breakfast, one before dinner, one before supper, and a final one when we went to bed. We never got drunk. But I will say that four times a day we were very genial. And when, in the middle of the cruise, Toddy was called back to San Francisco on business, Cloudesley and I saw to it that the Korean boy mixed toddies regularly for us according to formula.

But that was only on the boat. Back on the land, in my house, I took no before-breakfast eye-opener, no bed-going nightcap. And I have n't drunk hot toddies since, and that was many a year ago. But the point is, I *liked* those toddies. The geniality of which they were provocative was marvelous. They were eloquent proselyters for John Barleycorn in their small insidious way. They were tickles of the something destined to grow into daily and deadly desire. And I did n't know, never dreamed—I, who had lived with John Barleycorn for so many years and laughed at all his unavailing attempts to win me.

Chapter XXX

PART OF THE PROCESS of recovering from my long sickness was to find delight in little things, in things unconnected with books and problems, in play, in games of tag in the swimming pool, in flying kites, in fooling with horses, in working out mechanical puzzles. As a result, I grew tired of the city. On the ranch, in the Valley of the Moon, I found my paradise. I gave up living in cities. All the cities held for me were music, the theater, and Turkish baths.

And all went well with me. I worked hard, played hard, and was very happy. I read more fiction and less fact. I did not study a tithe as much as I had studied in the past. I still took an interest in the fundamental problems of existence, but it was a very cautious interest; for I had burned my fingers that time I clutched at the veils of Truth and rent them from her. There was a bit of lie in this attitude of mine, a bit of hypocrisy; but the lie and the hypocrisy were those of a man desiring to live. I deliberately blinded myself to what I took to be the savage interpretation of biological fact. After all, I was merely forswearing a bad habit, foregoing a bad frame of mind. And I repeat, I was very happy. And I add, that in all my days measuring them with cold, considerative judgment, this was, far and away beyond all other periods, the happiest period of my life.

But the time was at hand, rimeless and reasonless so far as I can see, when I was to begin to pay for my score of years of dallying with John Barleycorn. Occasionally guests journeyed to the ranch and remained a few days. Some did not drink. But to those who did drink, the absence of all alcohol on the ranch was a hardship. I could not violate my sense of hospitality by compelling them to endure this hardship. I ordered in a stock . . . for my guests.

I was never interested enough in cocktails to know how they were made. So I got a barkeeper in Oakland to make them in bulk and ship them to me. When I had no guests I did n't drink. But I began to notice, when I finished my morning's work, that I was glad if there were a guest, for then I could drink a cocktail with him.

Now I was so clean of alcohol that even a single cocktail was provocative of pitch. A single cocktail would glow the mind and tickle a laugh for the few minutes prior to sitting down to table and starting the delightful process of eating. On the other hand, such was the strength of my stomach, of my alcoholic resistance, that the single cocktail was only the glimmer of a glow, the faintest tickle of a laugh. One day a friend frankly and shamelessly suggested a second cocktail. I drank the second one with him. The glow was appreciably longer and warmer, the laughter deeper and more resonant. One does not forget such experiences. Sometimes I almost think that it was because I was so very happy that I started on my real drinking.

I remember one day Charmian and I took a long ride over the mountains on our horses. The servants had been dismissed for the day, and we returned late at night to a jolly chafing-dish supper. Oh, it was good to be alive that night while the supper was preparing, the two of us alone in the kitchen. I, personally, was at the top of life.

Such things as the books and ultimate truth did not exist. My body was gloriously healthy, and healthily tired from the long ride. It had been a splendid day. The night was splendid. I was with the woman who was my mate, picnicking in gleeful abandon. I had no troubles. The bills were all paid, and a surplus of money was rolling in on me. The future ever widened before me. And right there, in the kitchen, delicious things bubbled in the chafing dish, our laughter bubbled, and my stomach was keen with a most delicious edge of appetite.

I felt so good, that somehow, somewhere, in me arose an insatiable greed to feel better. I was so happy that I wanted to pitch my happiness even higher. And I knew the way. Ten thousand contacts with John Barleycorn had taught me. Several times I wandered out of the kitchen to the cocktail bottle, and each time I left it diminished by one man's size cocktail. The result was splendid. I was n't jingled, I was n't lighted up; but I was warmed, I glowed, my happiness was pyramided. Munificent as life was to me, I added to that munificence. It was a great hour—one of my greatest. But I paid for it, long afterwards, as you shall see. One does not forget such experiences, and, in human stupidity, cannot be brought to realize that there is no immutable law which decrees that same things shall produce same results. For they don't, else would the thousandth pipe of opium be provocative of similar delights to the first, else would one cocktail, instead of several, produce an equivalent glow after a year of cocktails.

One day, just before I ate midday dinner, after my morning's writing was done, when I had no guest, I took a cocktail by myself. Thereafter, when there were no guests, I took this daily pre-dinner cocktail. And right there John Barleycorn had me. I was beginning to drink regularly. I was beginning to drink alone. And I was beginning to drink, not for hospitality's sake, not for the sake of the taste, but for the effect of the drink.

I *wanted* that daily pre-dinner cocktail. And it never crossed my mind that there was any reason I should not have it. I paid for it. I could pay for a thousand cocktails each day if I wanted. And what was a cocktail—one cocktail—to me who on so many occasions for so many years had drunk inordinate quantities of stiffer stuff and been unharmed?

The program of my ranch life was as follows: Each morning, at eight-thirty, having been reading or correcting proofs in bed since four or five, I went to my desk. Odds and ends of correspondence and notes occupied me till nine, and at nine sharp, invariably, I began my writing. By eleven, sometimes a few minutes earlier or later, my thousand words were finished. Another half hour at cleaning up my desk, and my day's work was done, so that at eleven-thirty I got into a hammock under the trees with my mail bag and the morning newspaper. At twelve-thirty I ate dinner and in the afternoon I swam and rode.

One morning, at eleven-thirty, before I got into the hammock, I took a cocktail. I repeated this on subsequent mornings, of course, taking another cocktail just before I ate at twelve-thirty. Soon I found myself, seated at my desk in the midst of my thousand words, looking forward to that eleven-thirty cocktail.

At last, now, I was thoroughly conscious that I desired alcohol. But what of it? I was n't afraid of John Barleycorn. I had associated with him too long. I was wise in the matter of drink. I was discreet. Never again would I drink to excess. I knew the dangers and the pitfalls of John Barleycorn, the various ways by which he had tried to kill me in the past. But all that was past, long past. Never again would I drink myself to stupe-faction. Never again would I get drunk. All I wanted, and all I would take, was just enough to glow and warm me, to kick geniality alive in me and put laughter in my throat and stir the mag-gots of imagination slightly in my brain. Oh, I was thoroughly master of myself, and of John Barleycorn.

Chapter XXXI

BUT THE SAME STIMULUS to the human organism will not continue to produce the same response. By and by I discovered there was no kick at all in one cocktail. One cocktail left me dead. There was no glow, no laughter tickle. Two or three cocktails were required to produce the original effect of one. And I wanted that effect. I drank my first cocktail at eleven-thirty when I took the morning's mail into the hammock, and I drank my second cocktail an hour later just before I ate. I got into the habit of crawling out of the hammock ten minutes earlier so as to find time and decency for two more cocktails ere I ate. This became schedule—three cocktails in the hour that intervened between my desk and dinner. And these were two of the deadliest drinking habits: regular drinking and solitary drinking.

I was always willing to drink when any one was around. I drank by myself when no one was around. Then I made another step. When I had for guest a man of limited drinking caliber, I took two drinks to his one—one drink with him, the other drink without him and of which he did not know. I *stole* that other drink, and, worse than that, I began the habit of drinking alone when there was a guest, a man, a comrade, with whom I could have drunk. But John Barleycorn furnished the extenuation. It was a wrong thing to trip a guest up with excess of hospitality and get him drunk. If I persuaded him, with his limited caliber, into drinking up with me. I 'd surely get him drunk. What could I do but steal that every second drink, or else deny myself the kick equivalent to what he had got out of half the number?

Please remember, as I recite this development of my drinking, that I am no fool, no weakling. As the world measures such things, I am a success—I dare say a success more conspicuous than the success of the average successful man, and a success that required a pretty fair amount of brains and will power. My body is a strong body. It has survived where weaklings died like flies. And yet these things which I am relating happened to my body and to me. I am a fact. My drinking is a fact. My drinking is a thing that has happened, and is no theory nor speculation; and, as I see it, it but lays the emphasis on the power of John Barleycorn—a savagery that we still permit to exist, a deadly institution that lingers from the mad old brutal days and that takes its heavy toll of youth and strength and high spirit, and of very much of all of the best we breed.

To return. After a boisterous afternoon in the swimming pool, followed by a glorious ride on horseback over the mountains or up or down the Valley of the Moon, I found myself so keyed and splendid that I desired to be more highly keyed, to feel more splendid. I knew the way. A cocktail before supper was not the way. Two or three, at the very least, was what was needed. I took them. Why not? It was living. I had always dearly loved to live. This also became part of the daily schedule.

Then, too, I was perpetually finding excuses for extra cocktails. It might be the assembling of a particularly jolly crowd; a touch of anger against my architect or against a thieving stone-mason working on my barn; the death of my favorite horse in a barbed wire fence; or news of good

fortune in the morning mail from my dealings
with editors and publishers. It was immaterial
what the excuse might be, once the desire had
germinated in me. The thing was: I *wanted* alcohol. At last, after a score and more of years of
dallying and of not wanting, now I wanted it.
And my strength was my weakness. I required
two, three, or four drinks to get an effect com-
mensurate with the effect the average man got out
of one drink.

One rule I observed. I never took a drink until
my day's work of writing a thousand words was
done. And, when done, the cocktails reared a
wall of inhibition in my brain between the day's
work done and the rest of the day of fun to come.
My work ceased from my consciousness. No
thought of it flickered in my brain till next morning at nine o'clock when I sat at my desk and
began my next thousand words. This was a desirable condition of mind to achieve. I conserved my
energy by means of this alcoholic inhibition. John
Barleycorn was not so black as he was painted.
He did a fellow many a good turn, and this was
one of them.

And I turned out work that was healthful, and
wholesome, and sincere. It was never pessimistic.
The way to life I had learned in my long sickness.
I knew the illusions were right, and I exalted the
illusions. Oh, I still turn out the same sort of
work, stuff that is clean, alive, optimistic, and that
makes toward life. And I am always assured by
the critics of my superabundant and abounding
vitality, and of how thoroughly I am deluded by
these very illusions I exploit.

And while on this digression, let me repeat the
question I have repeated to myself ten thousand
times. *Why did I drink?* What need was there for
it? I was happy. Was it because I was too happy? I
was strong. Was it because I was too strong? Did I

possess too much vitality? I don't know why I drank. I cannot answer, though I can voice the suspicion that ever grows in me. I had been in too familiar contact with John Barleycorn through too many years. A left-handed man, by long practice, can become a right-handed man. Had I, a non-alcoholic, by long practice, become an alcoholic?

I was so happy! I had won through my long sickness to the satisfying love of woman. I earned more money with less endeavor. I glowed with health. I slept like a babe. I continued to write successful books, and in sociological controversy I saw my opponents confuted with the facts of the times that daily reared new buttresses to my intellectual position. From day's end to day's end I never knew sorrow, disappointment, nor regret. I was happy all the time. Life was one unending song. I begrudged the very hours of blessed sleep because by that much was I robbed of the joy that would have been mine had I remained awake. And yet I drank. And John Barleycorn, all unguessed by me, was setting the stage for a sickness all his own.

The more I drank the more I was required to drink to get an equivalent effect. When I left the Valley of the Moon, and went to the city and dined out, a cocktail served at table was a wan and worthless thing. There was no pre-dinner kick in it. On my way to dinner I was compelled to accumulate the kick—two cocktails, three, and, if I met some fellows, four or five, or six, it did n't matter within several. Once, I was in a rush. I had no time decently to accumulate the several drinks. A brilliant idea came to me. I told the barkeeper to mix me a double cocktail. Thereafter, whenever I was in a hurry, I ordered double cocktails. It saved time.

One result of this regular heavy drinking was to jade me. My mind grew so accustomed to spring

and liven by artificial means, that without artificial
means it refused to spring and liven. Alcohol became more and more imperative in order to meet
people, in order to become sociably fit. I had to
get the kick and the hit of the stuff, the crawl of
the maggots, the genial brain glow, the laughter
tickle, the touch of devilishness and sting, the
smile over the face of things, ere I could join my
fellows and make one with them.

Another result was that John Barleycorn was
beginning to trip me up. He was thrusting my
long sickness back upon me, inveigling me into
again pursuing Truth and snatching her veils away
from her, tricking me into looking reality stark in
the face. But this came on gradually. My thoughts
were growing harsh again, though they grew harsh
slowly.

Sometimes warnings crossed my mind. Where
was this steady drinking leading? But trust John
Barleycorn to silence such questions. "Come on
and have a drink and I'll tell you all about it," is
his way. And it works. For instance, the following
is a case in point, and one which John Barleycorn
never wearied of reminding me:

I had suffered an accident which required a
ticklish operation. One morning, a week after I
had come off the table, I lay on my hospital bed,
weak and weary. The sunburn of my face, what
little of it could be seen through a scraggly growth
of beard, had faded to a sickly yellow. My doctor
stood at my bedside on the verge of departure. He
glared disapprovingly at the cigarette I was smoking.

"That's what you ought to quit," he lectured.
"It will get you in the end. Look at me."

I looked. He was about my own age, broad-
shouldered, deep-chested, eyes sparkling, and
ruddy-cheeked with health. A finer specimen of
manhood one would not ask.

"I used to smoke," he went on. "Cigars. But I gave even them up. And look at me."

The man was arrogant, and rightly arrogant, with conscious well-being. And within a month he was dead. It was no accident. Half-a-dozen different bugs of long scientific names had attacked and destroyed him. The complications were astonishing and painful, and for days before he died the screams of agony of that splendid manhood could be heard for a block around. He died screaming.

"You see," said John Barleycorn. "He took care of himself. He even stopped smoking cigars. And that's what he got for it. Pretty rotten, eh? But the bugs will jump. There's no forefending them. Your magnificent doctor took every precaution, yet they got him. When the bug jumps you can't tell where it will land. It may be you. Look what he missed. Will you miss all I can give you, only to have a bug jump on you and drag you down? There is no equity in life. It's all a lottery. But I put the lying smile on the face of life and laugh at the facts. Smile with me and laugh. You 'll get yours in the end, but in the meantime laugh. It's a pretty dark world. I illuminate it for you. It's a rotten world, when things can happened such as happened to your doctor. There's only one thing to do; take another drink and forget it."

And of course I took another drink for the inhibition that accompanied it. I took another drink every time John Barleycorn reminded me of what had happened. Yet I drank rationally, intelligently. I saw to it that the quality of the stuff was of the best. I sought the kick and the inhibition, and avoided the penalties of poor quality and of drunkenness. It is to be remarked, in passing, that when a man begins to drink rationally and intelligently he betrays a grave symptom of how far along the road he has traveled.

But I continued to observe my rule of never taking my first drink of the day until the last word of my thousand words was written. On occasion, however, I took a day's vacation from my writing. At such times, since it was no violation of my rule, I did n't mind how early in the day I took that first drink. And persons who have never been through the drinking game wonder how the drinking habit grows!

Chapter XXXII

WHEN the *Snark* sailed on her long cruise from San Francisco there was nothing to drink on board. Or, rather, we were all of us unaware that there was anything to drink, nor did we discover it for many a month. This sailing with a "dry" boat was malice aforethought on my part. I had played John Barleycorn a trick. And it showed that I was listening ever so slightly to the faint warnings that were beginning to arise in my consciousness.

Of course, I veiled the situation to myself and excused myself to John Barleycorn. And I was very scientific about it. I said that I would drink only while in ports. During the dry sea-stretches my system would be cleansed of the alcohol that soaked it, so that when I reached a port I should be in shape to enjoy John Barleycorn more thoroughly. His bite would be sharper, his kick keener and more delicious.

We were twenty-seven days on the traverse between San Francisco and Honolulu. After the first day out, the thought of a drink never troubled me. This I take to show how intrinsically I am not an alcoholic. Sometimes, during the traverse, looking ahead and anticipating the delightful *lanai* luncheons and dinners of Hawaii (I had been there a couple of times before), I thought, naturally, of the drinks that would precede those meals. I did not think of those drinks with any yearning, with any irk at the length of the voyage. I merely thought they would be nice and jolly, part of the atmosphere of a proper meal.

Thus, once again I proved to my complete satisfaction that I was John Barleycorn's master. I could drink when I wanted, refrain when I wanted. Therefore I would continue to drink when I wanted.

Some five months were spent in the various islands of the Hawaiian group. Being ashore, I drank. I even drank a bit more than I had been accustomed to drink in California prior to the voyage. The people in Hawaii seemed to drink a bit more, on the average, than the people in more temperate latitudes. I do not intend the pun, and can awkwardly revise the statement to "latitudes more distant from the equator." Yet Hawaii is only sub-tropical. The deeper I got into the tropics the deeper I found men drank, the deeper I drank myself.

From Hawaii we sailed for the Marquesas. The traverse occupied sixty days. For sixty days we never raised land, a sail, nor a steamer smoke. But early in those sixty days, the cook, giving an overhauling to the galley, made a find. Down in the bottom of a deep locker he found a dozen bottles of angelica and muscatel. These had come down from the kitchen cellar of the ranch along with the home-preserved fruits and jellies. Six months in the galley-heat had effected some sort of a change in the thick sweet wine—brandied it, I imagine.

I took a taste. Delicious! And thereafter, once each day, at twelve o'clock, after our observations were worked up and the *Snark's* position charted, I drank half a tumbler of the stuff. It had a rare kick to it. It warmed the cockles of my geniality and put a fairer face on the truly fair face of the sea. Each morning, below, sweating out my thousand words, I found myself looking forward to that twelve o'clock event of the day.

The trouble was I had to share the stuff, and the length of the traverse was doubtful. I regretted that there were not more than a dozen bottles. And when they were gone I even regretted that I had shared any of it. I was thirsty for the alcohol, and eager to arrive in the Marquesas.

So it was that I reached the Marquesas the possessor of a real, man's size thirst. And in the Marquesas were several white men, a lot of sickly natives, much magnificent scenery, plenty of trade rum, an immense quantity of absinthe, but neither whisky nor gin. The trade rum scorched the skin of one's mouth. I know, because I tried it. But I had ever been plastic, and I accepted the absinthe. The trouble with the stuff was that I had to take such inordinate quantities in order to feel the slightest effect.

From the Marquesas I sailed with sufficient absinthe in ballast to last me to Tahiti, where I outfitted with Scotch and American whisky, and thereafter there were no dry stretches between ports. But please do not misunderstand. There was no drunkenness, as drunkenness is ordinarily understood—no staggering and rolling around, no befuddlement of the senses. The skilled and seasoned drinker, with a strong constitution, never descends to anything like that. He drinks to feel good, to get a pleasant jingle, and no more than that. The things he carefully avoids are the nausea of over-drinking, the after-effect of over-drinking, the helplessness and loss of pride of over-drinking.

What the skilled and seasoned drinker achieves is a discreet and canny semi-intoxication. And he does it by the twelve-month around without any apparent penalty. There are hundreds of thousands of men of this sort in the United States to-day, in clubs, hotels, and in their own homes—

men who are never drunk, and who, though most of them will indignantly deny it, are rarely sober. And all of them fondly believe, as I fondly believed, that they are beating the game.

On the sea-stretches I was fairly abstemious; but ashore I drank more. I seemed to need more, anyway, in the tropics. This is a common experience, for the excessive consumption of alcohol in the tropics by white men is a notorious fact. The tropics is no place for white-skinned men. Their skin-pigment does not protect them against the excessive white light of the sun. The ultra-violet rays, and other high-velocity and invisible rays from the upper end of the spectrum, rip and tear through their tissues, just as the X-ray ripped and tore through the tissues of so many laboratory experimenters before they learned the danger.

White men in the tropics undergo radical changes of nature. They become savage, merciless. They commit monstrous acts of cruelty that they would never dream of committing in their original temperate climate. They become nervous, irritable, and less moral. And they drink as they never drank before. Drinking is one form of the many forms of degeneration that set in when white men are exposed too long to too much white light. The increase of alcoholic consumption is automatic. The tropics is no place for a long sojourn. They seem doomed to die anyway, and the heavy drinking expedites the process. They don't reason about it. They just do it.

The sun-sickness got me, despite the fact that I had been in the tropics only a couple of years. I drank heavily during this time, but right here I wish to forestall misunderstanding. The drinking was not the cause of the sickness, nor of the abandonment of the voyage. I was strong as a bull, and for many months I fought the sun-sickness that was ripping and tearing my surface and nervous tissues to pieces. All through the New Hebrides and the Solomons and up among the atolls on the Line, during this period, under a tropic sun, rotten with malaria, and suffering from a few minor afflictions such as Biblical leprosy with the silvery skin, I did the work of five men.

To navigate a vessel through the reefs and shoals and passages and unlighted coasts of the coral seas is a man's work in itself. I was the only navigator on board. There was no one to check me up on the working out of my observations, nor any one with whom I could advise in the ticklish darkness among uncharted reefs and shoals. And I stood all watches. There was no seaman on board whom I could trust to stand a mate's watch. I was mate as well as captain. Twenty-four hours a day were the watches I stood at sea, catching cat-naps when I might. Third, I was doctor. And let me say right here that the doctor's job on the *Snark* at that time was a man's job. All on board suffered from malaria—the real, tropical malaria that can kill in three months. All on board suffered from perforating ulcers and from the maddening itch of *ngari ngari*. A Japanese cook went insane from his too numerous afflictions. One of my Polynesian sailors lay at death's door with blackwater fever. Oh, yes, it was a full man's job, and I dosed and doctored, and pulled teeth, and dragged my patients through mild little things like ptomaine poisoning.

Fourth, I was a writer. I sweated out my thousand words a day, every day, except when the shock of fever smote me, or a couple of nasty squalls smote the *Snark*, in the morning. Fifth, I was a traveler and a writer, eager to see things and to gather material into my note books. And, sixth, I was master and owner of the craft that was visiting strange places where visitors are rare and where visitors are made much of. So here I had to hold up the social end, entertain on board, be entertained ashore by planters, traders, governors, captains of war vessels, kinky-headed cannibal kings, and prime ministers sometimes fortunate enough to be clad in cotton under shirts.

Of course I drank. I drank with my guests and hosts. Also, I drank by myself. Doing the work of five men, I thought, entitled me to drink. Alcohol was good for a man who over-worked. I noted its effect on my small crew, when breaking their backs and hearts at heaving up anchor in forty fathoms, they knocked off gasping and trembling at the end of half an hour and had new life put into them by stiff jolts of rum. They caught their breaths, wiped their mouths, and went to it again with a will. And when we careened the *Snark* and had to work in the water to our necks between shocks of fever, I noted how raw trade-rum helped the work along.

And here again we come to another side of many-sided John Barleycorn. On the face of it, he gives something for nothing. Where no strength remains he finds new strength. The wearied one rises to greater effort. For the time being there is an actual accession of strength. I remember passing coal on an ocean steamer through eight days of hell, during which time we coal-passers were kept to the job by being fed whisky. We toiled half drunk all the time. And without the whisky we could not have passed the coal.

This strength John Barleycorn gives is not fictitious strength. It is real strength. But it is manufactured out of the sources of strength, and it must ultimately be paid for, and with interest. But what weary human will look so far ahead? He takes this apparently miraculous accession of strength at its face value. And many an over-worked business and professional man, as well as a harried common laborer, has traveled John Barleycorn's death-road because of this mistake.

Chapter XXXIII

I WENT to Australia to go into hospital and get tinkered up, after which I planned to go on with the voyage. And during the long weeks I lay in hospital, from the first day I never missed alcohol. I never thought about it. I knew I should have it again when I was on my feet. But when I regained my feet I was not cured of my major afflictions. Naaman's silvery skin was still mine. The mysterious sun-sickness, which the experts of Australia could not fathom, still ripped and tore my tissues. Malaria still festered in me and put me on my back in shivering delirium at the most unexpected moments, among other things compelling me to cancel a double lecture tour which had been arranged.

So I abandoned the *Snark* voyage and sought a cooler climate. The day I came out of hospital I took up drinking again as a matter of course. I drank wine at meals. I drank cocktails before meals. I drank Scotch highballs when anybody I chanced to be with was drinking them. I was so thoroughly the master of John Barleycorn, I could take up with him or let go of him whenever I pleased, just as I had done all my life.

After a time, for cooler climate, I went down to southern-most Tasmania in forty-three South. And I found myself in a place where there was nothing to drink. It did n't mean anything. I did n't drink. It was no hardship. I soaked in the cool air, rode horseback, and did my thousand words a day save when the fever shock came in the morning.

And for fear that the idea may still lurk in some minds that my preceding years of drinking were the cause of my disabilities, I here point out that my Japanese cabin-boy, Nakata, still with me, was rotten with fever, as was Charmian, who in addition was in the slough of a tropical neurasthenia that required several years of temperate climate to cure, and that neither she nor Nakata drank or ever had drunk.

When I returned to Hobart Town, where drink was obtainable, I drank as of old. The same when I arrived back in Australia. On the contrary, when I sailed from Australia on a tramp steamer commanded by an abstemious captain, I took no drink along, and had no drink for the forty-three days' passage. Arrived in Ecuador, squarely under the equatorial sun, where the humans were dying of yellow fever, smallpox, and the plague, I promptly drank again—every drink of every sort that had a kick in it. I caught none of these diseases. Neither did Charmian nor Nataka, who did not drink.

Enamored of the tropics, despite the damage done me, I stopped in various places, and was a long while getting back to the splendid, temperate climate of California. I did my thousand words a day, traveling or stopping over, suffered my last faint fever shock, saw my silvery skin vanish and my sun-torn tissues healthily knit again, and drank as a broad-shouldered, chesty man may drink.

Chapter XXXIV

BACK ON THE RANCH, in the Valley of the Moon, I resumed my steady drinking. My program was no drink in the morning; first drink-time came with the completion of my thousand words. Then, between that and the midday meal, were drinks numerous enough to develop a pleasant jingle. Again, in the hour preceding the evening meal, I developed another pleasant jingle. Nobody ever saw me drunk, for the simple reason that I never was drunk. But I did get a jingle twice each day; and the amount of alcohol I consumed every day, if loosed in the system of one unaccustomed to drink, would have put such a one on his back and out.

It was the old proposition. The more I drank, the more I was compelled to drink in order to get an effect. The time came when cocktails were inadequate. I had neither the time in which to drink them nor the space to accommodate them. Whisky had a more powerful jolt. It gave quicker action with less quantity. Bourbon or rye, or cunningly aged blends, constituted the pre-midday drinking. In the late afternoon it was Scotch and soda.

My sleep, always excellent, now became not quite so excellent. I had been accustomed to read myself back to sleep when I chanced to awake. But now this began to fail me. When I had read two or three of the small hours away and was as wide awake as ever, I found that a drink fur-

nished the soporific effect. Sometimes two or three
drinks were required.

So short a period of sleep then intervened before early morning rising, that my system did not
have time to work off the alcohol. As a result I
awoke with mouth parched and dry, with a slight
heaviness of head, and with a mild nervous palpi-
tation in the stomach. In fact I did not feel good. I
was suffering from the morning sickness of the
steady, heavy drinker. What I needed was a pick-
me-up, a bracer. Trust John Barleycorn, once he
has broken down a man's defenses! So it was a
drink before breakfast to put me right for breakfast—
the old poison of the snake that has bitten one!
Another custom, begun at this time, was that of
the pitcher of water by the bed-side to furnish
relief to my scorched and sizzling membranes.

I achieved a condition in which my body was
never free from alcohol. Nor did I permit myself
to be away from alcohol. If I traveled to out-of-the-
way places, I declined to run the risk of finding
them dry. I took a quart, or several quarts, along
in my grip. In the past I had been amazed by
other men guilty of this practice. Now I did it
myself unblushingly. And when I got out with
the fellows, I cast all rules by the board. I drank
when they drank, what they drank, and in the
same way they drank.

I was carrying a beautiful alcoholic conflagra-
tion around with me. The thing fed on its own
heat and flamed the fiercer. There was no time, in
all my waking time, that I did n't want a drink. I
began to anticipate the completion of my daily
thousand words by taking a drink when only five
hundred words were written. It was not long until I prefaced the beginning of the thousand words
with a drink.

The gravity of this I realized too well. I made
new rules. Resolutely I would refrain from drink-

ing until my work was done. But a new and most diabolical complication arose. The work refused to be done without drinking. It just could n't be done. I had to drink in order to do it. I was beginning to fight now. I had the craving at last, and it was mastering me. I would sit at my desk and dally with pad and pen, but words refused to flow. My brain could not think the proper thoughts because continually it was obsessed with the one thought that across the room in the liquor cabinet stood John Barleycorn. When, in despair, I took my drink, at once my brain loosened up and began to roll off the thousand words.

In my town house, in Oakland, I finished the stock of liquor and wilfully refused to purchase more. It was no use, because, unfortunately, there remained in the bottom of the liquor cabinet a case of beer. In vain I tried to write. Now beer is a poor substitute for strong waters; beside, I did n't like beer; yet all I could think of was that beer so singularly accessible in the bottom of the cabinet. Not until I had drunk a pint of it did the words begin to reel off, and the thousand were reeled off to the tune of numerous pints. The worst of it was that the beer caused me severe heart-burn; but despite the discomfort I soon finished the case.

The liquor cabinet was now bare. I did not replenish it. By truly heroic perseverance, I finally forced myself to write the daily thousand words without the spur of John Barleycorn. But all the time I wrote I was keenly aware of the craving for a drink. And as soon as the morning's work was done, I was out of the house and away down-town to get my first drink. Merciful goodness!—if John Barleycorn could get such sway over me, a non-alcoholic, what must be the sufferings of the true alcoholic, battling against the organic demands of his chemistry while those closest to him sympathize little, understand less, and despise and deride him!

Chapter XXXV

B UT THE FREIGHT has to be paid. John Barleycorn began to collect, and he collected not so much from the body as from the mind. The old long sickness, which had been purely an intellectual sickness, recrudesced. The old ghosts, long laid, lifted their heads again. But they were different and more deadly ghosts. The old ghosts, intellectual in their inception, had been laid by a sane and normal logic. But now they were raised by the White Logic of John Barleycorn, and John Barleycorn never lays the ghosts of his raising. For this sickness of pessimism, caused by drink, one must drink further in quest of the anodyne that John Barleycorn promises but never delivers.

How to describe this White Logic to those who have never experienced it? It is perhaps better first to state how impossible such a description is. Take Hasheesh Land, for instance, the land of enormous extensions of time and space. In past years I have made two memorable journeys into that far land. My adventures there are seared in sharpest detail on my brain. Yet I have tried vainly, with endless words, to describe any tiny particular phase to persons who have not traveled there.

I used all the hyperbole of metaphor, and tell what centuries of time and profounds of unthinkable agony and horror can obtain in each interval of all the intervals between the notes of a quick jig played quickly on the piano. I talk for an hour, elaborating that one phase of Hasheesh Land, and at the end I have told them nothing. And when I cannot tell them this one thing of all the vastness of terrible and wonderful things, I know I have failed to give them the slightest concept of Hasheesh Land.

But, let me talk with some other traveler in that weird region, and at once am I understood. A phrase, a word, conveys instantly to his mind what hours of words and phrases could not convey to the mind of the non-traveler. So it is with John Barleycorn's realm where the White Logic reigns. To those untraveled there, the traveler's account must always seem unintelligible and fantastic. At the best, I may only beg of the untraveled ones to strive to take on faith the narrative I shall relate.

For there are fatal intuitions of truth that reside in alcohol. Philip sober vouches for Philip drunk in this matter. There seem to be various orders of truth in this world. Some sorts of truth are truer than others. Some sorts of truth are lies, and these sorts are the very ones that have the greatest use-value to life that desires to realize and live. At once, O untraveled reader, you see how lunatic and blasphemous is the realm I am trying to describe to you in the language of John Barleycorn's tribe. It is not the language of your tribe, all of whose members resolutely shun the roads that lead to death and tread only the roads that lead to life. For there are roads and roads, and of truth there are orders and orders. But have patience. At least, through what seems no more than verbal yammerings, you may, perchance, glimpse faint far vistas of other lands and tribes.

Alcohol tells truth, but its truth is not normal. What is normal is healthful. What is healthful tends toward life. Normal truth is a different order, and a lesser order, of truth. Take a dray horse. Through all the vicissitudes of its life, from first to last, somehow, in unguessably dim ways, it must believe that life is good; that the drudgery in harness is good; that death, no matter how blind-instinctively apprehended, is a dread giant; that life is beneficent and worth-while; that, in the end, with fading life, it will not be knocked about and beaten and urged beyond its sprained and spavined best; that old age, even, is decent, dignified, and valuable, though old age means a ribby scarecrow in a hawker's cart, stumbling a step to every blow, stumbling dizzily on through merciless servitude and slow disintegration to the end— the end, the apportionment of its parts (of its subtle flesh, its pink and springy bone, its juices and ferments, and all the sensateness that informed it), to the chicken farm, the hide-house, the glue-rendering works, and the bone-meal fertilizer factory. To the last stumble of its stumbling end this dray horse must abide by the mandates of the lesser truth that is the truth of life and that makes life possible to persist.

This dray horse, like all other horses, like all other animals including man, is life-blinded and sense-struck. It will live, no matter what the price. The game of life is good, though all of life may be hurt, and though all lives lose the game in the end. This is the order of truth that obtains, not for the universe, but for the live things in it if they for a little space will endure ere they pass. This order of truth, no matter how erroneous it may be, is the sane and normal order of truth, the rational order of truth that life must believe in order to live.

To man, alone among the animals, has been given the awful privilege of reason. Man, with his brain, can penetrate the intoxicating show of things and look upon a universe brazen with indifference toward him and his dreams. He can do this, but it is not well for him to do it. To live, and live abundantly, to sting with life, to be alive (which is to be what he is), it is good that man be life-blinded and sense-struck. What is good is true. And this is the order of truth, lesser though it be, that man must know and guide his actions by, with unswerving certitude that it is absolute truth and that in the universe no other order of truth can obtain. It is good that man should accept at face value the cheats of sense and snares of flesh, and through the fogs of sentiency pursue the lures and lies of passion. It is good that he shall see neither shadows nor futilities, nor be appalled by his lusts and rapacities.

And man does this. Countless men have glimpsed that other and truer order of truth and recoiled from it. Countless men have passed through the long sickness and lived to tell of it and deliberately to forget it to the end of their days. They lived. They realized life, for life is what they were. They did right.

And now comes John Barleycorn with the curse he lays upon the imaginative man who is lusty with life and desire to live. John Barleycorn sends his White Logic, the argent messenger of truth beyond truth, the antithesis of life, cruel and bleak as interstellar space, pulseless and frozen as absolute zero, dazzling with the frost of irrefragable logic and unforgettable fact. John Barleycorn will not let the dreamer dream, the liver live. He destroys birth and death, and dissipates to mist the paradox of being, until his victim cries out, as in "The City of Dreadful Night": "Our life's a cheat, our death a black abyss." And the feet of the victim of such dreadful intimacy take hold of the way of death.

Chapter XXXVI

BACK to personal experiences and the effects in the past of John Barleycorn's White Logic on me. On my lovely ranch in the Valley of the Moon, brain-soaked with many months of alcohol, I am oppressed by the cosmic sadness that has always been the heritage of man. In vain do I ask myself why I should be sad. My nights are warm. My roof does not leak. I have food galore for all the caprices of appetite. Every creature-comfort is mine. In my body are no aches nor pains. The good old flesh-machine is running smoothly on. Neither brain nor muscle is overworked. I have land, money, power, recognition from the world, a consciousness that I do my meed of good in serving others, a mate whom I love, children that are of my own fond flesh. I have done, and am doing, what a good citizen of the world should do. I have built houses, many houses, and tilled many a hundred acres. And as for trees, have I not planted a hundred thousand? Everywhere, from any window of my house, I can gaze forth upon these trees of my planting, standing valiantly erect and aspiring toward the sun.

My life has indeed fallen in pleasant places. Not a hundred men in a million have been so lucky as I. Yet, with all this vast good fortune, am I sad. And I am sad because John Barleycorn is with me. And John Barleycorn is with me because I was born in what future ages will call the dark ages before the ages of rational civilization. John Barleycorn is with me because in all the unwitting days of my youth John Barleycorn was accessible, calling to me and inviting me on every corner and on every street between the corners. The pseudo-civilization into which I was born permitted everywhere licensed shops for the sale of soul-poison. The system of life was so organized that I (and millions like me) was lured and drawn and driven to the poison shops.

Wander with me through one mood of the myriad of moods of sadness into which one is plunged by John Barleycorn. I ride out over my beautiful ranch. Between my legs is a beautiful horse. The air is wine. The grapes on a score of rolling hills are red with autumn flame. Across Sonoma Mountain wisps of sea fog are stealing. The afternoon sun smoulders in the drowsy sky. I have everything to make me glad I am alive. I am filled with dreams and mysteries. I am all sun and air and sparkle. I am vitalized, organic. I move, I have the power of movement, I command movement of the live thing I bestride. I am possessed with the pomps of being, and know proud passions and inspirations. I have ten thousand august connotations. I am a king in the kingdom of sense, and trample the face of the uncomplaining dust. . . .

And yet, with jaundiced eye I gaze upon all the beauty and wonder about me, and with jaundiced brain consider the pitiful figure I cut in this world that endured so long without me and that will again endure without me. I remember the men who broke their hearts and their backs over this stubborn soil that now belongs to me. As if anything imperishable could belong to the perishable! These men passed. I, too, shall pass. These men toiled, and cleared, and planted, gazed with aching eyes, while they rested their labor-stiffened bodies, on these same sunrises and sunsets, at the autumn glory of the grape, and at the fog-wisps stealing across the mountain. And they are gone. And I know that I, too, shall some day, and soon, be gone.

Gone? I am going now. In my jaw are cunning artifices of the dentists which replace the parts of me already gone. Never again will I have the thumbs of my youth. Old fights and wrestlings have injured them irreparably. That punch on the head of a man whose very name is forgotten, settled this thumb finally and forever. A slip-grip at catch-as-catch-can did for the other. My lean runner's stomach has passed into the limbo of memory. The joints of the legs that bear me up are not so adequate as they once were, when, in wild nights and days of toil and frolic, I strained and snapped and ruptured them. Never again can I swing dizzily aloft and trust all the proud quick that is I to a single rope-clutch in the driving blackness of storm. Never again can I run with the sled-dogs along the endless miles of Arctic trail.

I am aware that within this disintegrating body which has been dying since I was born I carry a skeleton; that under the rind of flesh which is called my face is a bony, noseless death's head. All of which does not shudder me. To be afraid is to be healthy. Fear of death makes for life. But the curse of the White Logic is that it does not make one afraid. The world-sickness of the White Logic makes one grin jocosely into the face of the Noseless One and to sneer at all the phantasmagoria of living.

I look about me as I ride, and on every hand I see the merciless and infinite waste of natural selection. The White Logic insists upon opening the long-closed books, and by paragraph and chapter states the beauty and wonder I behold in terms of futility and dust. About me is murmur and hum, and I know it for the gnat-swarm of the living, piping for a little space its thin plaint of troubled air.

I return across the ranch. Twilight is on, and the hunting-animals are out. I watch the piteous tragic play of life feeding on life. Here is no morality. Only in man is morality, and man created it— a code of action that makes toward living and that is of the lesser order of truth. Yet all this I knew before, in the weary days of my long sickness. These were the greater truths that I so successfully schooled myself to forget; the truths that were so serious that I refused to take them seriously, and played with gently, O so gently, as sleeping dogs at the back of consciousness which I did not care to waken. I did but stir them, and let them lie. I was too wise, too wicked wise, to wake them. But now White Logic willy nilly wakes them for me, for White Logic, most valiant, is unafraid of all the monsters of the earthly dream.

"Let the doctors of all the schools condemn me," White Logic whispers as I ride along. "What of it? I am truth. You know it. You cannot combat me. They say I make for death. What of it? It is truth. Life lies in order to live. Life is a perpetual lie-telling process. Life is a mad dance in the domain of flux, wherein appearances in mighty tides ebb and flow, chained to the wheels of moons beyond our ken. Appearances are ghosts. Life is ghost land, where appearances change, transfuse, permeate each the other and all the others, that are, that are not, that always flicker, fade, and pass, only to come again as new appearances, as other appearances. You are such an appearance, composed of countless appearances out of the past. All an appearance can know is mirage. You know mirages of desire. These very mirages are the unthinkable and incalculable congeries of appearances that crowd in upon you and form you out of the past, and that sweep you on to dissemination into other unthinkable and incalculable congeries of appearances to people the ghost land of the future. Life is apparitional, and passes. You are an apparition. Through all the apparitions that preceded you and that compose the parts of you, you rose gibbering from the evolutionary mire, and gibbering you will pass on, interfusing, permeating the procession of apparitions that will succeed you."

And of course it is all unanswerable, and as I ride along through the evening shadows I sneer at the Great Fetish which Comte called the world. And I remember what another pessimist of sentiency has uttered: "Transient are all. They being born, must die; and, being dead, are glad to be at rest."

But here through the dusk comes one who is not glad to be at rest. He is a workman on the ranch, an old man, an immigrant Italian. He takes his hat off to me in all servility, because, forsooth, I am to him a lord of life. I am food to him, and shelter, and existence. He has toiled like a beast all his days, and lived less comfortably than my horses in their deep-strawed stalls. He is labor-crippled. He shambles as he walks. One shoulder is twisted higher than the other. His hands are gnarled claws, repulsive, horrible. As an apparition he is a pretty miserable specimen. His brain is as stupid as his body is ugly.

"His brain is so stupid that he does not know he is an apparition," the White Logic chuckles to me. "He is sense-drunk. He is the slave of the dream of life. His brain is filled with superrational sanctions and obsessions. He believes in a transcendent over-world. He has listened to the vagaries of the prophets, who have blown for him the sumptuous bubble of Paradise. He feels inarticulate affinities with self-conjured non-realities. He sees penumbral visions of himself titubating fantastically through days and nights of space and stars. Beyond the shadow of any doubt he is convinced that the universe was made for him, and that it is his destiny to live forever in the immaterial and supersensuous realms he and his kind have builded of the stuff of semblance and deception.

"But you, who have opened the books and who share my awful confidence—you know him for what he is, brother to you and the dust, a cosmic joke, a sport of chemistry, a garmented beast that arose out of the ruck of screaming beastliness by virtue and accident of two opposable great toes. He is brother as well to the gorilla and the chimpanzee. He thumps his chest in anger, and roars and quivers with cataleptic ferocity. He knows monstrous, atavistic promptings, and he is composed of all manner of shreds of abysmal and forgotten instincts."

"Yet he dreams he is immortal," I argue feebly. "It is vastly wonderful for so stupid a clod to bestride the shoulders of time and ride the eternities."

"Pah!" is the retort. "Would you then shut the books and exchange places with this thing that is only an appetite and a desire, a marionette of the belly and the loins?"

"To be stupid is to be happy," I contend.

"Then your ideal of happiness is a jelly-like organism floating in a tideless, tepid, twilight sea, eh?"

—Oh, the victim cannot combat John Barleycorn!

"One step removed from the annihilating bliss of Buddah's Nirvana," the White Logic adds. "Oh, well, here's the house. Cheer up and take a drink. We know, we illuminated, you and I, all the folly and the farce."

And in my book-walled den, the mausoleum of the thoughts of men, I take my drink, and other drinks, and roust out the sleeping dogs from the recesses of my brain and halloo them on over the walls of prejudice and law and through all the cunning labyrinths of superstition and belief.

"Drink," says the White Logic. "The Greeks believed that the gods gave them wine so that they might forget the miserableness of existence. And remember what Heine said."

Well do I remember that flaming Jew's "With the last breath all is done: joy, love, sorrow, macaroni, the theater, lime-trees, raspberry drops, the power of human relations, gossip, the barking of dogs, champagne."

"Your clear white light is sickness," I tell the White Logic. "You lie."

"By telling too strong a truth," he quips back.

"Alas, yes, so topsyturvy is existence," I acknowledge sadly.

"Ah, well, Liu Ling was wiser than you," the White Logic girds. "You remember him?"

I nod my head—Liu Ling, a hard drinker, one of the group of bibulous poets who called themselves the Seven Sages of the Bamboo Grove and who lived in China many an ancient century ago.

"It was Liu Ling," prompts the White Logic, "who declared that to a drunken man the affairs of this world appear but as so much duckweed on a river. Very well. Have another Scotch, and let semblance and deception become duckweed on a river."

And while I pour and sip my Scotch, I remember another Chinese philosopher, Chuang Tzu, who, four centuries before Christ, challenged this dreamland of the world, saying: "How then do I know but that the dead repent of having previously clung to life? Those who dream of the banquet, wake to lamentation and sorrow. Those who dream of lamentation and sorrow, wake to join the hunt. While they dream, they do not know that they dream. Some will even interpret the very dream they are dreaming; and only when they awake do they know it was a dream. . . . Fools think they are awake now, and flatter themselves they know if they are really princes or peasants. Confucius and you are both dreams; and I who say you are dreams—I am but a dream myself.

"Once upon a time, I, Chuang Tzu, dreamt I was a butterfly fluttering hither and thither, to all intents and purposes a butterfly. I was conscious only of following my fancies as a butterfly, and was unconscious of my individuality as a man. Suddenly, I awaked, and there I lay, myself again. Now I do not know whether I was then a man dreaming I was a butterfly, or whether I am now a butterfly dreaming I am a man."

Chapter XXXVII

"COME," says the White Logic, "and forget these Asian dreamers of old time. Fill your glass and let us look at the parchments of the dreamers of yesterday who dreamed their dreams on your own warm hills."

I pore over the abstract of title of the vineyard called Tokay on the rancho called Petaluma. It is a sad long list of the names of men, beginning with Manuel Micheltoreno, one time Mexican "Governor, Commander-in-Chief, and Inspector of the Department of the Californias," who deeded ten square leagues of stolen Indian land to Colonel Don Mariano Guadalupe Vallejo for services rendered his country and for moneys paid by him for ten years to his soldiers.

Immediately this musty record of man's land-lust assumes the formidableness of a battle—the quick struggling with the dust. There are deeds of trust, mortgages, certificates of release, transfers, judgments, foreclosures, writs of attachment, orders of sale, tax liens, petitions for letters of administration, and decrees of distribution. It is like a monster ever unsubdued, this stubborn land that drowses in this Indian summer weather and that survives them all, the men who scratched its surface and passed.

Who was this James King of William, so curiously named? The oldest surviving settler in the Valley of the Moon knows him not. Yet only sixty years ago he loaned Mariano G. Vallejo eighteen thousand dollars on security of certain lands including the vineyard yet to be and to be called Tokay. Whence came Peter O'Connor, and whither vanished, after writing his little name of a day on the woodland that was to become a vineyard? Appears Louis Csomortanyi, a name to conjure with. He lasts through several pages of this record of the enduring soil.

Comes old American stock, thirsting across the Great American Desert, mule-backing across the Isthmus, wind-jamming around the Horn, to write brief and forgotten names where ten thousand generations of wild Indians are equally forgotten—names like Halleck, Hastings, Swett, Tait, Denman, Tracy, Grimwood, Carlton, Temple. There are no names like those to-day in the Valley of the Moon.

The names begin to appear fast and furiously, flashing from legal page to legal page and in a flash vanishing. But ever the persistent soil remains for others to scrawl themselves across. Come the names of men of whom I have vaguely heard but whom I have never known. Kohler and Frohling— who built the great stone winery on the vineyard called Tokay, but who built upon a hill up which other vinyardists refused to haul their grapes. So Kohler and Frohling lost the land; the earthquake of 1906 threw down the winery; and I now live in its ruins.

La Motte—he broke the soil, planted vines and orchards, instituted commercial fish-culture, built a mansion renowned in its day, was defeated by the soil, and passed. And my name of a day appears. On the site of his orchards and vineyards, of his proud mansion, of his very fish ponds, I have scrawled myself with a hundred thousand eucalyptus trees.

Cooper and Greenlaw—on what is called the Hill Ranch they left two of their dead, "Little

JOHN BARLEYCORN   225

Lillie" and "Little David," who rest to-day inside
a tiny square of hand-hewn palings. Also, Cooper
and Greenlaw in their time cleared the virgin for-
est from three fields of forty acres. To-day I have
those three fields sown with Canada peas, and in
the spring they shall be plowed under for green
manure.

Haska—a dim legendary figure of a generation
ago, who went back up the mountain and cleared
six acres of brush in the tiny valley that took his
name. He broke the soil, reared stone walls and a
house, and planted apple trees. And already the
site of the house is undiscoverable, the location of
the stone walls may be deduced from the configu-
ration of the landscape, and I am renewing the
battle, putting in Angora goats to browse away
the brush that has overrun Haska's clearing and
choked Haska's apple trees to death. So I, too,
scratch the land with my brief endeavor and flash
my name across a page of legal script ere I pass
and the page grows musty.

"Dreamers and ghosts," the White Logic chuckles.

"But surely the striving was not altogether vain,"
I contend.

"It was based on illusion and is a lie."

"A vital lie," I retort.

"And pray what is a vital lie but a lie?" the
White Logic challenges. "Come. Fill your glass
and let us examine these vital liars who crowd
your bookshelves. Let us dabble in William James
a bit."

"A man of health," I say. "From him we may
expect no philosopher's stone, but at least we
shall find a few robust tonic things to which to
tie."

"Rationality gelded to sentiment," the White
Logic grins. "At the end of all his thinking he still
clung to the sentiment of immortality. Facts transmuted in the alembic of hope into terms of faith.

The ripest fruit of reason the stultification of reason. From the topmost peak of reason James teaches to cease reasoning and to have faith that all is well and will be well—the old, oh, ancient old, acrobatic flip of the metaphysicians whereby they reasoned reason quite away in order to escape the pessimism consequent upon the grim and honest exercise of reason.

"Is this flesh of yours you? Or is it an extraneous something possessed by you? Your body—what is it? A machine for converting stimuli into reactions. Stimuli and reactions are remembered. They constitute experience. Then you are in your consciousness these experiences. You are at any moment what you are thinking at that moment. Your I is both subject and object; it predicates things of itself and is the things predicated. The thinker is the thought, the knower is what is known, the possessor is the things possessed.

"After all, as you know well, man is a flux of states of consciousness, a flow of passing thoughts, each thought of self another self, a myriad thoughts, a myriad selves, a continual becoming but never being, a will-of-the-wisp flitting of ghosts in ghostland. But this, man will not accept of himself. He refuses to accept his own passing. He will not pass. He will live again if he has to die to do it.

"He shuffles atoms and jets of light, remotest nebulæ, drips of water, prick-points of sensation, slime-oozings and cosmic bulks, all mixed with pearls of faith, love of woman, imagined dignities, frightened surmises, and pompous arrogances, and of the stuff builds himself an immortality to startle the heavens and baffle the immensities. He squirms on his dunghill, and like a child lost in the dark among goblins, calls to the gods that he is their younger brother, a prisoner of the quick that is destined to be as free as they—monuments of egotism reared by the epiphenomena; dreams and the dust of dreams, that vanish when the dreamer vanishes and are no more when he is not.

"It is nothing new, these vital lies men tell themselves, muttering and mumbling them like charms and incantations against the powers of Night. The voodoos and medicine men and the devil-devil doctors were the fathers of metaphysics. Night and the Noseless One were ogres that beset the way of light and life. And the metaphysicians would win by if they had to tell lies to do it. They were vexed by the brazen law of the Ecclesiast that men die like the beasts of the field and their end is the same. Their creeds were their schemes, their religions their nostrums, their philosophies their devices, by which they half-believed they would outwit the Noseless One and the Night.

"Bog-lights, vapors of mysticism, psychic overtones, soul orgies, wailings among the shadows, weird gnosticisms, veils and tissues of words, gibbering subjectivisms, gropings and maunderings, ontological fantasies, pan-psychic hallucinations—this is the stuff, the phantasms of hope, that fills your book shelves. Look at them, all the sad wraiths of sad mad men and passionate rebels—your Schopenhauers, your Strindbergs, your Tolstois and Nietzsches.

"Come. Your glass is empty. Fill and forget."

I obey, for my brain is now well a-crawl with the maggots of alcohol, and as I drink to the sad thinkers on my shelves I quote Richard Hovey:

"Abstain not! Life and Love, like night and day,
Offer themselves to us on their own terms,
    Not ours. Accept their bounty while ye may,
Before we be accepted by the worms."

"I will cap you," cries the White Logic.
"No," I answer, while the maggots madden

me. "I know you for what you are, and I am
unafraid. Under your mask of hedonism you are
yourself the Noseless One and your way leads to
the Night. Hedonism has no meaning. It, too, is a
lie, at best the coward's smug compromise—"

"Now will I cap you!" the White Logic breaks in.

> "But if you would not this poor life fulfil,
> Lo, you are free to end it when you will,
> Without the fear of waking after death."

And I laugh my defiance; for now, and for the
moment, I know the White Logic to be the arch-
impostor of them all, whispering his whispers of
death. And he is guilty of his own unmasking,
with his own genial chemistry turning the tables
on himself, with his own maggots biting alive the
old illusions, resurrecting and making to sound
again the old voice from beyond of my youth,
telling me again that still are mine the possibilities
and powers which life and the books had taught
me did not exist.

And the dinner-gong sounds to the reversed
bottom of my glass. Jeering at the White Logic, I
go out to join my guests at table, and with as-
sumed seriousness to discuss the current magazines and the silly doings of the world's day,
whipping every trick and ruse of controversy
through all the paces of paradox and persiflage.
And, when the whim changes, it is most easy and
delightfully disconcerting to play with the respect-
able and cowardly bourgeois fetishes and to laugh
and epigram at the flitting god-ghosts and the
debaucheries and follies of wisdom.

The clown's the thing! The clown! If one must
be a philosopher, let him be Aristophanes. And
no one at the table thinks I am jingled. I am in
fine fettle, that is all. I tire of the labor of thinking,
and, when the table is finished, start practical

jokes and set all playing at games, which we carry on with bucolic boisterousness.

And when the evening is over and good night said, I go back through my book-walled den to my sleeping porch and to myself and to the White Logic which, undefeated, has never left me. And as I fall to fuddled sleep I hear Youth crying, as Harry Kemp heard it:

"I heard Youth calling in the night:
'Gone is my former world-delight;
For there is naught my feet may stay;
The morn suffuses into day,
It dare not stand a moment still
But must the world with light fulfil.
More evanescent than the rose
My sudden rainbow comes and goes
Plunging bright ends across the sky—
Yea, I am Youth because I die!' "

Chapter XXXVIII

THE FOREGOING is a sample roaming with the
White Logic through the dusk of my soul. To the
best of my power I have striven to give the reader
a glimpse of a man's secret dwelling when it is
shared with John Barleycorn. And the reader must
remember that this mood, which he has read in a
quarter of an hour, is but one mood of the myriad
moods of John Barleycorn, and that the procession of such moods may well last the clock around
through many a day and week and month.

My alcoholic reminiscences draw to a close. I
can say, as any strong, chesty drinker can say,
that all that leaves me alive to-day on the planet is
my unmerited luck—the luck of chest, and shoulders, and constitution. I dare to say that a not
large percentage of youths, in the formative stage
of fifteen to seventeen, could have survived the
stress of heavy drinking that I survived between
my fifteenth and seventeenth years; that a not
large percentage of men could have punished the
alcohol I have punished in my manhood years
and lived to tell the tale. I survived, through no
personal virtue, but because I did not have the
chemistry of a dipsomaniac and because I possessed an organism unusually resistant to the rav-
ages of John Barleycorn. And, surviving, I have
watched the others die, not so lucky, down all the
long sad road.

It was my unmitigated and absolute good for-

tune, good luck, chance, call it what you will, that
brought me through the fires of John Barleycorn.
My life, my career, my joy in living, have not
been destroyed. They have been scorched, it is
true; but, like the survivors of forlorn hopes, they
have by unthinkably miraculous ways come through
the fight to marvel at the tally of the slain.

And like such a survivor of old red War who
cries out, "Let there be no more war!" so I cry
out, "Let there be no more poison-fighting by our
youths!" The way to stop war is to stop it. The
way to stop drinking is to stop it. The way China
stopped the general use of opium was by stopping the cultivation and importation of opium.
The philosophers, priests, and doctors of China
could have preached themselves breathless against
opium for a thousand years, and the use of opium,
so long as opium was ever-accessible and obtainable, would have continued unabated. We are so
made, that is all. We have with great success
made a practice of not leaving arsenic and strych-
nine, and typhoid and tuberculosis germs, lying
around for our children to be destroyed by. Treat
John Barleycorn the same way. Stop him. Don't
let him lie around, licensed and legal, to pounce
upon our youth. Not of alcoholics nor for alcoholics do I write, but for our youths, for those who
possess no more than the adventure-stings and
the genial predispositions, the social man-impulses,
which are twisted all awry by our barbarian civilization which feeds them poison on all the corners. It is the healthy, normal boys, now born or
being born, for whom I write.

It was for this reason, more than any other, and
more ardently than any other, that I rode down
into the Valley of the Moon, all a-jingle, and voted
for equal suffrage. I voted that women might vote,
because I knew that they, the wives and mothers
of the race, would vote John Barleycorn out of

existence and back into the historical limbo of our vanished customs of savagery. If I thus seem to cry out as one hurt, please remember that I have been sorely bruised and that I do dislike the thought that any son or daughter of mine or yours should be similarly bruised.

The women are the true conservators of the race. The men are the wastrels, the adventure-lovers and gamblers, and in the end it is by their women that they are saved. About man's first experiment in chemistry was the making of alcohol, and down all the generations to this day man has continued to manufacture and drink it. And there has never been a day when the women have not resented man's use of alcohol, though they have never had the power to give weight to their resentment. The moment women get the vote in any community, the first thing they proceed to do, or try to do, is to close the saloons. In a thousand generations to come men of themselves will not close the saloons. As well expect the morphine victims to legislate the sale of morphine out of existence.

The women know. They have paid an incalculable price of sweat and tears for man's use of alcohol. Ever jealous for the race, they will legislate for the babes of boys yet to be born; and for the babes of girls, too, for they must be the mothers, wives, and sisters of these boys.

And it will be easy. The only ones that will be hurt will be the topers and seasoned drinkers of a single generation. I am one of these, and I make solemn assurance, based upon long traffic with John Barleycorn, that it won't hurt me very much to stop drinking when no one else drinks and when no drink is obtainable. On the other hand, the overwhelming proportion of young men are so normally non-alcoholic, that, never having had access to alcohol, they will never miss it. They will know of the saloon only in the pages of history, and they will think of the saloon as a quaint old custom similar to bull-baiting and the burning of witches.

Chapter XXXIX

OF COURSE, no personal tale is complete without bringing the narrative of the person down to the last moment. But mine is no tale of a reformed drunkard. I was never a drunkard, and I have not reformed.

It chanced, some time ago, that I made a voyage of one hundred and forty-eight days in a windjammer around the Horn. I took no private supply of alcohol along, and though there was no day of those one hundred and forty-eight days that I could not have got a drink from the captain, I did not take a drink. I did not take a drink because I did not desire a drink. No one else drank on board. The atmosphere for drinking was not present, and in my system there was no organic need for alcohol. My chemistry did not demand alcohol.

So there arose before me a problem, a clear and simple problem: *This is so easy, why not keep it up when you get back on land?* I weighed this problem carefully. I weighed it for five months, in a state of absolute non-contact with alcohol. And out of the data of past experience, I reached certain conclusions.

In the first place, I am convinced that not one man in ten thousand, or in a hundred thousand, is a genuine, chemical dipsomaniac. Drinking, as I deem it, is practically entirely a habit of mind. It is unlike tobacco, or cocaine, or morphine, or all the rest of the long list of drugs. The desire for alcohol is quite peculiarly mental in its origin. It is a matter of mental training and growth, and it is cultivated in a social soil. Not one drinker in a million began drinking alone. All drinkers begin socially, and this drinking is accompanied by a thousand social connotations such as I have described out of my own experience in the first part of this narrative. These social connotations are the stuff of which the drink habit is largely composed. The part that alcohol itself plays is inconsiderable, when compared with the part played by the social atmosphere in which it is drunk. The human is rarely born these days, who, without long training in the social relations of drinking, feels the irresistible chemical propulsion of his system toward alcohol. I do assume that such rare individuals are born, but I have never encountered one.

On this long, five-months' voyage, I found that among all my bodily needs not the slightest shred of a bodily need for alcohol existed. But this I did find: my need was mental and social. When I thought of alcohol, the connotation was fellowship. When I thought of fellowship, the connotation was alcohol. Fellowship and alcohol were Siamese twins. They always occurred linked together.

Thus, when reading my in desk-chair or when talking with others, practically any mention of any part of the world I knew instantly aroused the connotation of drinking and good fellows. Big nights and days and moments, all purple passages and freedoms, thronged my memory. "Venice" stares at me from the printed page, and I remember the café tables on the sidewalks. "The Battle of Santiago," some one says, and I answer, "Yes, I 've been over the ground." But I do not see the ground, nor Kettle Hill, nor the Peace Tree. What I see is the Café Venus, on the plaza of Santiago, where one hot night I talked long and drank deep with a dying consumptive.

The East End of London, I read, or some one says; and first of all, under my eyelids, leap the visions of the shining pubs, and in my ears echo the calls for "two of bitter" and "three of Scotch." The Latin Quarter—at once I am in the student cabarets, bright faces and keen spirits around me, sipping cool, well-dripped absinthe while our voices mount and soar in Latin fashion as we settle God and art and democracy and the rest of the simple problems of existence.

In a pampero off the River Plate, we speculate, if we are disabled, of running in to Buenos Ayres, the "Paris of America," and I have visions of bright congregating-places of men, of the jollity of raised glasses, and of song and cheer and the hum of genial voices. When we have picked up the Northeast Trades in the Pacific, we try to persuade our dying captain to run for Honolulu, and while I persuade I see myself again drinking cocktails on the cool *lanais*, and fizzes out at Waikiki where the surf rolls in. Some one mentions the way wild ducks are cooked in the restaurants of San Francisco, and at once I am transported to the light and clatter of many tables, where I gaze at old friends across the golden brims of long-stemmed Rhine-wine glasses.

And so I pondered my problem. I should not care to revisit all these fair places of the world except in the fashion I visited them before. *Glass in hand!* There is a magic in the phrase. It means more than all the words in the dictionary can be made to mean. It is a habit of mind to which I have been trained all my life. It is now part of the stuff that composes me. I like the bubbling play of wit, the chesty laughs, the resonant voices of men, when, glass in hand, they shut the gray world outside and prod their brains with the fun and folly of an accelerated pulse.

No, I decided; I shall take my drink on occa-

sion. With all the books on my shelves, with all
the thoughts of the thinkers shaded by my particular temperament, I decided coolly and deliberately that I should continue to do what I had been
trained to want to do. I would drink—but, oh,
more skillfully, more discreetly, than ever before.
Never again would I be a peripatetic conflagra-
tion. Never again would I invoke the White Logic.
I had learned how not to invoke him.

The White Logic now lies decently buried alongside the Long Sickness. Neither will afflict me
again. It is many a year since I laid the Long
Sickness away; his sleep is sound. And just as
sound is the sleep of the White Logic. And yet, in
conclusion, I can well say that I wish my forefa-
thers had banished John Barleycorn before my
time. I regret that John Barleycorn flourished everywhere in the system of society in which I was
born, else I should not have made his acquaintance, and I was long trained in his acquaintance.

ℂ

Renowned American Literature in SIGNET CLASSIC Editions

(0451)

☐ **JOHN BARLEYCORN, OR, ALCOHOLIC MEMOIRS by Jack London.** An autobiographical masterpiece of intense emotional power, and an unsparing social commentary on the evils of drink.   (524284—$3.95)

☐ **SELECTED WRITINGS OF RALPH WALDO EMERSON.** Foreword by William H. Gilman, University of Rochester. Fourteen essays and addresses including *The Oversoul, Politics, Thoreau,* and *Divinity School Address,* poetry including *Threnody* and *Uriel* and selections from his letters and journals. Chronology. Bibliography.   (524047—$4.95)

☐ **EVANGELINE and Selected Tales and Poems by Henry Wadsworth Longfellow.** Edited by Horace Gregory, poet and translator. Also includes *The Whitnesses, The Courtship of Miles Standish,* and selections from *Hiawatha.* Commentaries on Longfellow by Van Wyck Brooks, Norman Holmes Pearson, and Lewis Carroll. Includes Introduction, Bibliography and Chronology.   (520033—$3.95)

☐ **LEAVES OF GRASS by Walt Whitman.** Introduction by Gay Wilson Allen, New York University. The text of this edition is that of the "Deathbed," or 9th edition, published in 1892. The content and grouping of the poems were authorized by the poet for this final and complete edition of his masterpiece. Index and Bibliography included.   (517024—$2.95)

☐ **WALDEN and ON THE DUTY OF CIVIL DISOBEDIENCE by Henry David Thoreau.** Afterword by Perry Miller, author of *The Puritan Mind.* Also includes a selection of poetry, *Sic Vita, Winter Memories, To The Maiden in the East, Smoke, Mist,* and *Inspiration.*   (523776—$2.50)

Prices slightly higher in Canada

STORIES BY MARK TWAIN

☐ **ADVENTURES OF TOM SAWYER.** Here is a light-hearted excursion into boyhood, a nostalgic return to the simple, rural Missouri world of Tom Sawyer and his friends Huck Finn, Becky and Aunt Polly. There is sheer delight in *Tom Sawyer*—even at the darkest moments affection and wit permeate its pages.   (523555—$1.95)

☐ **ADVENTURES OF HUCKLEBERRY FINN.** Rich in color, humor and the adventurous frontier experience of the Mississippi, this great novel vividly recreates the world, the people and the language that Mark Twain knew and loved from his own years on the riverboats. (519124—$1.75)

☐ **LIFE ON THE MISSISSIPPI.** At once a romantic history of a mighty river, an autobiographical account of Twain's early steamboat days, and a storehouse of humorous anecdotes and sketches, it is an epochal record of America's vanished past that earned for its author his first recognition as a serious writer.   (521722—$2.50)

☐ **A CONNECTICUT YANKEE IN KING ARTHUR'S COURT.** Hank Morgan, cracked on the head by a crowbar in the nineteenth-century Connecticut, wakes to find himself in King Arthur's England, facing a world whose idyllic surface masks fear, injustice, and ignorance. The grim truths of Twain's Camelot strike a resounding contemporary note. (523539—$2.25)

Prices slightly higher in Canada

Buy them at your local

bookstore or use coupon

on next page for ordering.

HORROR AND HIGH ADVENTURE

☐ **PHANTOM OF THE OPERA by Gaston Leroux** (521730—$3.95)

☐ **THE CELESTIAL RAILROAD And Other Stories by Nathaniel Hawthorne.** Afterword by R. P. Blackmur. (522133—$3.50)

☐ **THE MARBLE FAUN by Nathaniel Hawthorne.** Afterword by Murray Krieger. (009030—$3.95)

☐ **THE SCARLET LETTER by Nathaniel Hawthorne.** Foreword by Leo Marx. (523504—$1.75)

☐ **THE HOUSE OF THE SEVEN GABLES by Nathaniel Hawthorne.** Afterword by Edward C. Sampson. (523091—$2.50)

☐ **THE FALL OF THE HOUSE OF USHER AND OTHER TALES by Edgar Allan Poe.** Afterword by R. P. Blackmur. (521749—$2.95)

☐ **CALL OF THE WILD AND SELECTED STORIES by Jack London.** Foreword by Franklin Walker. (523164—$2.25)

☐ **THE SEA WOLF AND SELECTED STORIES by Jack London.** Afterword by Franklin Walker. (523563—$2.25)

☐ **MOBY DICK by Herman Melville.** Afterword by Denham Sutcliffe. (520211—$2.25)

☐ **BILLY BUDD AND OTHER TALES by Herman Melville.** Afterword by Willard Thorp. (522370—$2.50)

☐ **THE CONFIDENCE MAN by Herman Melville.** Afterword by R. W. B. Lewis. (008948—$4.95)

☐ **PIERRE or THE AMBIGUITIES by Herman Melville.** Afterword by Lawrence Thompson. (518969—$4.95)

☐ **TYPEE by Herman Melville.** Afterword by Harrison Hayford. (522494—$3.95)

☐ **WHITE JACKET by Herman Melville.** Introduction by Alfred Kazin. (009553—$4.95)

☐ **MUTINY ON THE BOUNTY by William Bligh.** (522931—$3.50)

Prices slightly higher in Canada